BIG ROCK

by Lauren Blakely

ALSO BY LAUREN BLAKELY

The Caught Up in Love Series (Each book in this series follows a different couple so each book can be read separately, or enjoyed as a series since characters crossover)

Caught Up in Her (A short prequel novella to
    Caught Up in Us)
Caught Up In Us
Pretending He's Mine
Trophy Husband
Stars in Their Eyes

Standalone Novels

BIG ROCK
Mister Orgasm (2016)
Far Too Tempting
21 Stolen Kisses
Playing With Her Heart (A standalone SEDUCTIVE
    NIGHTS spin-off novel about Jill and Davis)

The No Regrets Series

The Thrill of It
The Start of Us
Every Second With You

The Seductive Nights Series

First Night (Julia and Clay, prequel novella)
Night After Night (Julia and Clay, book one)
After This Night (Julia and Clay, book two)
One More Night (Julia and Clay, book three)

Nights With Him (A standalone novel about Michelle and Jack)
Forbidden Nights (A standalone novel about Nate and Casey)

The Sinful Nights Series

Sweet Sinful Nights
Sinful Desire
Sinful Longing
Sinful Love (2016)

The Fighting Fire Series

Burn For Me (Smith and Jamie)
Melt for Him (Megan and Becker)
Consumed By You (Travis and Cara)

The Sapphire Affair
A two-book series releasing Summer 2016

ABOUT

It's not just the motion of the ocean, ladies. It's definitely the SIZE of the boat too.

And I've got both firing on all cylinders. In fact, I have ALL the right assets. Looks, brains, my own money, and a big cock.

You might think I'm an asshole. I sound like one, don't I? I'm hot as sin, rich as heaven, smart as hell and hung like a horse.

Guess what? You haven't heard my story before. Sure, I might be a playboy, like the NY gossip rags call me. But I'm the playboy who's actually a great guy. Which makes me one of a kind.

The only trouble is, my dad needs me to cool it for a bit. With conservative investors in town wanting to buy his flagship Fifth Avenue jewelry store, he needs me not only to zip it up, but to look the part of the committed guy. Fine. I can do this for Dad. After all, I've got him to thank for the family jewels. So I ask my best friend and business partner to be my fiancée for the next week. Charlotte's up for it. She has her own reasons for saying yes to wearing this big rock.

And pretty soon all this playing pretend in public leads to no pretending whatsoever in the bedroom, because she just can't fake the kind of toe-curling, window-shattering orgasmic cries she makes as I take her to new heights between the sheets.

But I can't seem to fake that I might be feeling something real for her.

What the fuck have I gotten myself into with this...big rock?

DEDICATION

This book is dedicated to Helen Williams because of the day I messaged you and asked if you could make an R look like a C. You nailed that, Helen, and that's why this book exists. And, as always, to my dear friend Cynthia.

PROLOGUE

My dick is fucking awesome.

But don't just take my word for it. Consider all its accomplishments.

First, let's start with the obvious one.

Size.

Sure, some people will tell you that size does not matter. You know what I'll tell you? *They lie.*

You don't want a tiny diamond on your finger when you can have three carats. You don't want a one-dollar bill when you can have a Benjamin. And you don't want to ride a miniature pony when you can saddle up on a rock-star cock at the rodeo of your pleasure.

Why? Because bigger is better. It's more fun. Ask any woman who's ever had to utter the dreaded words, "Is it in yet?"

No woman has ever had to ask me that.

You're probably wondering by now—just how big is it? C'mon. A gentleman doesn't tell. I may fuck like a god, but I'm still a gentleman. I'll open your door before I open your legs. I'll hold your coat for you, I'll pay for dinner, and I'll treat you like a queen in and out of bed.

But I get it. You want an image in your mind. A measurement in inches to make your mouth water. Fine. Imagine this. Picture your fantasy-sized cock; mine's fucking bigger.

Moving on to looks. Let's be honest. Some dicks are just motherfucking ugly. I won't get into all the reasons why. You know what they are, and when it comes to my best asset, all I want you thinking about are these words: long, thick, smooth, hard. If the Renaissance masters were carving sculptures of cocks, mine would be the model for all of them.

But honestly, none of this would matter if my dick didn't possess the most important attribute of all.

Performance.

Ultimately, a man's dick should be measured by the number of orgasms it delivers. I'm not talking about the solo flights. That's cheating. I'm talking about the Os that can make a woman's back arch, her toes curl, her windows shatter... Her world rock.

How much pleasure has my dick wrought? I don't kiss and tell, but I'll leave you with this. My dick has a perfect track record.

That's why it fucking sucks that he has to go on hiatus.

CHAPTER ONE

Men don't understand women.

That's just a fact of life.

Like that guy.

The dude down there at the corner of my bar. His elbow's on the metal counter in an *aren't I casual and cool* pose. He's stroking his handlebar mustache, and he's acting like he's the best listener in the world as he talks to a hot brunette with square red glasses. But the thing is, he's staring at her rack.

Fine, the brunette has nice tits. And I mean "nice" in the sense that they could occupy their own zip code.

But c'mon, man.

Her eyes are up there. And you've got to look at them, or the lady is going to walk.

I finish pouring a pale ale for one of our regulars, a businessman who pops in once a week. He's working the whole *my boss sucks for making me travel* look, and at the very least I can help him in the drink department.

"This one's on the house. Enjoy," I say, sliding the glass to him.

"Best news I've had all day," he says with a small quirk of the lips, before he chugs half the glass and plunks down a three-dollar tip. Nice. The bartenders here, who depend on tips, will appreciate it. But Jenny had to take off early because her sister had some sort of crisis, so I'm handling the last of the customers, while my business partner, Charlotte, is managing the books.

As Handlebar leans in closer to Red Square, she backs away, shakes her head, grabs her purse, and heads for the exit.

Yup. I could be a fortuneteller if my specialty was predicting when a man would score and when he wouldn't. Most of the time, the odds are definitely not in the dude's favor, because he makes the most common bar mistakes. Like starting the conversation with a stupid pick-up line. *"Girl, you make my software turn into hardware,"* or *"You should sell hot dogs because you sure know how to make a weiner stand."* Yeah I couldn't believe my ears either. Or how about this mistake? The guy who has a wandering eye and can't stop checking out the other attractions. What woman is going to find that flattering?

The worst bar sin, though, is *assuming.* Assuming she wants to talk to you. Assuming she's going home with you. Assuming you can kiss her without her permission.

You know what they say happens when you assume.

But me?

Just check my diploma. I double majored in college with one degree in finance and the other in the language of women—and I graduated summa cum laude. I have an encyclopedic understanding of what a woman wants…and giving it to her. I achieved full fluency in female body language, the clues, and the gestures.

Like right now.

Charlotte is tapping away on her laptop and biting the corner of her lip in concentration. Translation: *I am on a roll, so do not bother me or I will throat punch you.*

Okay, fine. She's not really a throat-puncher. But the point being, she is giving off major Do Not Disturb vibes.

Handlebar, though, can't read, speak, or write Woman. He's sauntering along the bar, getting ready to make a move. Thinking he's got a chance with her.

From my spot behind the bar, wiping down glasses, I can practically hear him clearing his throat as he preps to say hello to Charlotte.

I can understand why the man has my best friend in his crosshairs. Charlotte is pretty much a goddess of the highest order. First, she has wavy, blonde hair, paired with deep brown eyes. Most blondes have blue eyes, so Charlotte gets major points for the killer reverse combo that just slams you with its unexpected and absolute hotness.

Next, she possesses a fantastic dry sense of humor.

Plus, she's whip smart.

But Handlebar doesn't know those last two. He's only aware that she's gorgeous, so he's about to make his play. He snags the stool next to her and flashes a toothy grin. She flinches, startled that this guy just invaded her blinders-on work zone.

Charlotte can totally handle herself. But we made a pact long ago, and re-upped when we went into business together on this bar. If either of us needs a fake girlfriend or boyfriend to gracefully get out of a sticky situation, we've sworn to step in and act the part.

It's a game we've played since college, and it works like a charm.

It also works because Charlotte and I would never be a real couple. I need her too much as a friend, and judging from the number of times she's laughed with me, or cried on my shoulder, she needs me too. Which is another reason why this tactic is brilliant—we both know we will never be more than friends.

I walk around the bar and head straight for Charlotte, right as Handlebar reaches her and says his name, then asks for hers.

I slide in and brush a hand on her lower back, as if she's mine. As if I'm the one who gets to touch this body, thread his fingers through her hair, and look into those eyes. I tilt my head and flash him the biggest shit-eating grin, because I'm the lucky son-of-a-bitch who goes home with her in this scenario. "My fiancée's name is Charlotte. Nice to meet you. I'm Spencer," I say, and offer a hand to shake.

The guy wrinkles his nose like a rabbit, getting a clue that he's just struck out again tonight.

"Have a good night," he mutters, and scurries out.

Charlotte tips her chin to me and gives an approving nod. "Look at you. Captain Fiancé coming to the rescue," she says, running a hand along my arm and squeezing my bicep. "I didn't even see him making the moves."

"That's why you've got me. I have eyes everywhere," I say as I lock the front door. The bar is empty now. It's just us, like it's been so many nights at closing time.

"And usually those peepers are busy scanning for available women," she says, shooting me an *I know you so well* stare.

"What can I say? I like to give my eyes a good workout, too—just like the rest of me," I say, patting my flat as a board belly.

Then she yawns.

"Get to bed," I tell her.

"You should, too. Oh, wait. You probably have a date."

She's not far off. I usually do.

Earlier this month, I met a total babe at the gym. She worked out hard, then worked out even harder with me when I bent her over the back of the couch in my apartment. She texted me the next day, telling me how her thighs were aching, and she'd loved it. She said if I ever made it to Los Angeles, would I please look her up, because she wanted to ride my ride again.

Of course she did. Once you've had filet mignon, you don't want to go back to hamburger helper.

I saved her number. You never know, right? Nothing wrong with two adults enjoying the night and parting ways in the morning with a spring in the step courtesy of multiple Os bestowed.

That's how it should be. The first rule of dating is this—always please the woman first, then ideally a second time before you get yours in. The next two are equally simple—don't get attached, and never, ever be a douche. I follow my own rules, and they have given me the good life. I'm twenty-eight, single, rich, hot, and a gentleman. Like it's a surprise when I get laid.

But tonight, my dick is off duty. Early bedtime.

I shake my head in answer to Charlotte's question as I resume cleaning the counters. "Nah, I have a seven-thirty breakfast tomorrow with my dad and some guy he's trying to sell the store to. I need to be fresh and ready to impress."

She points to the door. "Go get your beauty sleep, Spencer. I'll close up."

"I don't think so. I came to fill in for Jenny. You go home. I'll hail you a cab."

"You do know I've lived in New York for five years, right? I know how to hail a cab late at night."

"I am well aware of your independent ways. But I don't care—I'm sending you home. Whatever you're doing here, you can do at your apartment," I tell her as I toss the washrag in the sink. "Wait. You're not worried that Bradley Dipstick is going to be roaming around the lobby trying to give you flowers at this time of night?"

"No. He usually plans his apology ambushes for the daylight hours. Yesterday, he sent me a three-foot-tall teddy bear holding a red satin heart that said, *Please forgive me.* What the hell am I supposed to do with that?"

"Send it back to him. At his office. With red lipstick on the heart spelling out N.O." Charlotte's ex-boyfriend is a grade A, top-choice douchenozzle, and the bastard will never get her back. I hold up a hand. "Wait. Is there any chance this teddy bear has a middle finger on his paw?"

She laughs. "Now that's a good idea. I just wish the whole building didn't know my business."

"I know. I wish you didn't have to run into him ever again in the whole history of time."

I hail her a cab, give her a peck on the cheek, and send her home. After I close up, I head to my pad in the West Village—the sixth floor of a kickass brownstone with a terrace that has a view of all lower Manhattan. Perfect on a June night like this.

I toss my keys on the entryway table as I scroll through my recent messages on my phone. I laugh when my sister Harper texts me a photo from a gossip mag, one from a few weeks ago, of me out with the hot woman from the gym. Turns out she's a celebrity trainer from some reality TV show. And I'm the *"noted New York City playboy"*—same thing the magazine called me when I was seen with a hot new chef at a restaurant opening in Miami last month.

Tonight, I'm a good boy though.

I make no promises for tomorrow.

CHAPTER TWO

Button-down shirt. Tie. Charcoal-gray pants. Dark brown hair, green eyes, chiseled jaw.

Yep, it's all working.

I fully approve of myself this Friday morning, and if I were a dude in a cheesy movie, I'd give myself two thumbs up.

But honestly, I'm not that kind of guy. I mean, who does that?

Instead, I turn to my cat, Fido, and ask him what he thinks. His response is simple—he struts off in the other direction, his tail high in the air.

Fido and I have an understanding: I feed him, and he doesn't cock-block me. He'd appeared on my balcony a year ago, meowing at the sliding glass door, wearing a tag that said "Princess Poppy." I checked his collar, and found he belonged to this sweet little old lady in the building who'd just moved on to the Great Beyond. That sweet little old lady had, evidently, confused him for a girl. She'd left no relatives, nor any forwarding instructions for the cat. I took him in, ditched his pink sparkly collar, and gave him a name befitting his manhood.

It's a win-win relationship.

Like tomorrow night. Fido won't bitch and moan when I come home late. Because I fully expect to be stumbling through the door in the wee hours. I'm working tonight, but Jenny's back on shift tomorrow, and I need to take my man Nick out to celebrate. His hit TV show was just re-upped for another season on Comedy Nation, and we plan to toast many times over at a watering hole in Gramercy Park. Besides, there's a hot bartender there I've talked to a few times. Her name is Lena, and she makes a mean Harvey Wallbanger, so she put her name in my contacts as the drink itself. Well, part of the drink. *Bang Her.*

Sounds promising enough, and by promising I mean, a sure thing.

I take off and make my way uptown on the subway to the Upper East Side, my parents' stomping ground. Yeah, they're well off, but they're also—shocker—not assholes. That's right. This isn't the story of a guy with a rich, shithead dad and a cold, bitchy mom. This is the tale of a guy who likes his parents and whose parents like him. Guess what else? My parents like each other, too.

How do I know this?

Because I'm not fucking deaf. No, I didn't hear *that* when I was a kid. Instead, I heard my mom whistling a happy tune every morning when she woke up. I learned some good lessons from them. Happy wife = happy life, and one way to make a woman happy is in the bedroom.

Today though, my job is to make Dad happy, and Dad wants his offspring with him at this breakfast meeting, including my little sister, Harper. She walks toward me on

Eighty-Second Street, her red hair like a sheet of flame. When she reaches me, she pretends she's about to take a quarter from behind my ear.

"Look what I found. Wait. What's that here?" She waves her hand behind my other ear and produces a tampon.

Her mouth falls into a shocked *O*. "Spencer Holiday. You're carrying tampons now? When did you start getting your period?"

I crack up.

She reaches behind my other ear, and brandishes a small pill. "Oh look, here's some Advil for when you get cramps."

"Good one." I smile. "Do you perform that one at all the children's parties?"

"No." Harper winks. "But it's tricks like that that keep the moms booking me six months out."

She joins me as we walk toward the restaurant on Third Avenue, wandering along one of those perfect New York blocks—the kind with wide stoops, and red brick brownstones, and trees with lush branches every ten feet. It looks like the set of a rom-com.

"How's the city's noted playboy? I heard Cassidy Winters said you were the best time she's had in ages."

I furrow my brow. "Who's that?"

She rolls her eyes. "The hot trainer you were in the papers with. I sent you the picture last night. Didn't you read the caption?"

I shake my head. "Nah. Besides, she was ages ago." That's what a few weeks feels like in the dating world.

"Guess she's still singing your praises."

"Looks like I'll be erasing her number." Flapping your gums will get you blackballed.

"Well, you better watch it with Mr. Offerman. Dad's buyer," she says, as a blue-haired lady walking a Pomeranian heads in our direction.

"You mean I shouldn't hit on him?" I ask, deadpan. I stop in the middle of the block. Gyrate my hips. Give my best stripper stare. "Do a little dance." I smack my own ass. "Back it up."

Harper's face goes beet red. She shifts her eyes in the direction of the lady. "Oh my god. Stop it."

"So, don't do my usual Chippendales' routine, then?"

She grabs my arm, and pulls me along as we pass the dog owner. The woman waggles her eyebrows at me, and mouths, "Nice moves."

See? Chicks dig me.

"Anyway, what I mean is, he's very conservative. Family values and all. Which is why we're here."

"Of course. Act as if we're a happy family and like each other. Right? Is that what I should do?" I say and give her a huge noogie. Because she deserves it.

"Ouch. Don't mess up my hair."

"Fine, fine. I get it. You want me to pretend I'm a choirboy and you're an angel."

She places her palms together in prayer. "I *am* an angel."

We enter the restaurant, and my dad greets us in the lobby. Harper excuses herself for the ladies' room, and my dad claps me on the back. "Thank you for joining me. You got the memo, right?"

"Of course. Don't I look the part of the successful, blue-blooded son?" I slide my hand along my tie, courtesy of Barneys, thank you very much.

He gives me a mock punch on the jaw. "You always do." Then he drapes an arm over my shoulders. "Ah, I'm so glad you're here. And listen," he says, lowering his voice, "you know I don't care what you do after hours. But Mr. Offerman has four daughters, ages seventeen down to eleven. So he prefers a bit more of a—"

"Goody Two-shoes image?" I say, flashing my best good-boy grin.

My dad snaps his fingers and nods.

"Are they here at breakfast? His daughters?"

He shakes his head. "Just you and your sister, him and me. He wanted to meet the two of you. And all I mean is the less your status as the '*noted New York City playboy*' comes up, the happier he will be, and the happier he is, the happier I am. Can you do that?"

I heave a sigh and widen my eyes. "I don't know, Dad. That, like, seriously limits my conversational abilities. Since I usually only talk about women and sex. Fuck," I say in a frustrated tone. I pretend to prop myself up, counting off on my fingers. "Okay, politics, religion, gun control. That's what I'll focus on, 'kay?"

"Don't make me get my muzzle," he jokes.

"Dad, I got this. I will not derail your dream. I promise you that. For the next hour, I am the dutiful son and rising New York businessman. I won't say a word about women, or the Boyfriend Material app," I tell him, because I'm a chameleon. I can play party boy or serious businessman. I can play Yale graduate or trash talker. Today, I'll be calling on my Ivy League self, not the dude who created and sold one of the hottest dating apps.

"Thank you for keeping low-key about that side of things. I've been searching for years for the right buyer, and I think we've finally found one. If all goes well on the last few details, we should be signing the papers the end of next week."

My dad is a rock star in the jewelry business. Hardly anyone knows his name, but pretty much everyone knows his store. He started Katharine's on Fifth Avenue thirty years ago, and it is the definition of class in the jewelry business. The sky blue boxes the store uses have become nothing short of iconic—a sign that a gorgeous gift is on its way. Pearls, diamonds, rubies, silver, gold—you name it. Named for my mom, Katharine's is a palace of sophistication, and my dad has turned the Fifth Avenue store into the flagship of a chain with locations in twelve cities around the globe. Katharine's put my sister and me through private school, then college, and has generally made our lives all-around awesome.

Dad wants to retire and sail around the world with my mom. It's been his dream, and he finally found the right buyer, someone who gets the refined elegance he's built, and has the financial profile for the kind of transaction he requires.

Leaving the business to Harper or me was never in the cards. I have zero interest in running an international jewelry chain, and my sister doesn't either. I'm already doing what I love—running the three Lucky Spot bars in Manhattan with Charlotte. Besides, I made my own mint when I launched Boyfriend Material straight out of college.

The whole premise was simple, but genius.

No dick pics allowed.

Because – wait for it – women don't like dick pics. At the early stage of dating, there's basically nothing more aggressive and off-putting than sending a lady you're interested in a shot of your junk. Doesn't matter if you're hung like a horse—that shot will make her cringe. My app offered a haven for women, a promise that they wouldn't be photographically assaulted by unwelcome cock shots.

The app took off, my investors made major bank, and I cleaned up like the lucky bastard I am.

But for the next hour, while talking to Mr. Offerman, I'm simply a guy who works in the food and beverage business. Game on.

CHAPTER THREE

Dad escorts Harper and me to a big round table, covered in a crisp white tablecloth, in the back of the restaurant.

"Mr. Offerman, I'm delighted to introduce you to my children. This is my daughter Harper, and my son Spencer."

With dark eyes and jet-black hair, Mr. Offerman is tall and imposing. He's built like a tree trunk, and he stands ramrod straight. I bet he was military. He has the air of a general.

"Pleasure to meet the two of you," he says in a deep baritone. Yup, this man gives orders.

We exchange pleasantries and settle in at the table. Once we order, he narrows in on Harper.

"I've heard a lot about you. How fantastic that you're a magician…" As he pumps her with questions, it hits me—Harper's profession is perfect for his "family-friendly" image. She works kids' parties, and he's eating that up. She shows him some of her tricks. She makes his fork disappear, then his napkin, then his water glass.

"Wonderful. I bet it simply mesmerizes all the children. My girls would love that."

Dude, you have teenagers. I highly doubt they're keen on sleight of hand.

"I'll be happy to show them," Harper says, bestowing her shining smile on Mr. Offerman, winning him over.

"Wonderful. I'd love to set up a dinner for tomorrow night for all of us. With my wife and daughters."

"I'd love to be there," Harper says.

He fixes his gaze on me. "And how is Boyfriend Material going?"

Ah, there it is. Clearly he's done his research. "I hear from the company that bought it that it's going well. But I'm not involved anymore," I say, deflecting the question.

"It's quite a hit, from what I read about it. You seem to know what women want."

I gulp and hazard a glance at my dad. He has on his plastic smile. He doesn't want Mr. Offerman going down this road. "All I know, sir, is that you need to treat a woman well, and when the time is right to get down on one knee, you should go for more than one carat from Katharine's." I give myself props for the jewelry joke.

He smiles and nods, then clears his throat. "I also have a reporter from *Metropolis Life and Times* magazine that's following the sale of the jewelry franchise. Bit of a business feature—bit of a lifestyle piece, too. I hope it's not too much to ask, but I'd love if we can all agree to focus on the stores over the next few weeks during the transition. Not on matchmaking apps or related matters that the press seems to love. Like dating *exploits*." He stops to spread his napkin across his lap. "Do you know what I mean?"

We all know what you mean, man.

My father weighs in. "I couldn't agree more. There's no need for the article to be about anything else but jewelry."

"Good." Mr. Offerman returns his focus to me, and the inquisition isn't over. "Your new business is going well?"

"The food and beverage industry is a fantastic one to be in. Charlotte and I started The Lucky Spot three years ago, and it's going great. Fun place, great reviews, customers are happy."

He peppers me with more questions about the bar, and I can tell it's all part of his need to vet me in person. To see if my new business seems as "sleazy" as he thinks my last one was. But I can handle men like him. I didn't start my own company because I was easily intimidated. I started it because I was fucking fearless, and I read the market, just like I can read him. I know how to give him what he wants, and I do so with each answer because giving him what he wants is good for my dad.

"What do you enjoy most about it?"

"Working with Charlotte is great," I say, because how can I go wrong with that answer? "We were pretty much meant to do this together. We see eye to eye on everything."

A smile tugs at the corner of his lips. "That's fantastic. How long have you—" His question is cut off when the waiter brings our plates, but I've got the gist of it. *How long have we been friends...*

"Since college," I answer.

"Wonderful," he says, as the waiter sets down his eggs benedict. "I hope you can join us tomorrow night for the dinner party, then."

Oh, so I've passed his test. Yay me.

"I'd be thrilled," I say.

There goes celebrating with Nick. But he'll understand. I sneak a glance at my dad, who's looking pleased that this breakfast is going well so far.

Mr. Offerman picks up his fork. "And perhaps you could bring your girlfriend."

I nearly choke on my orange juice.

My dad starts to correct him, but Mr. Offerman keeps talking, that big baritone leaving no room for interruption. "My wife would love to meet Charlotte. All my girls would, too. We have such a family-centric business, and it's so important to maintain that during a visible transition time, considering the media interest and all. I love knowing that they'll see this committed side of you"

I part my lips to correct the misunderstanding. To tell him Charlotte is just a friend. That we're only business partners.

But his smile right now is like his signature on the deal itself. I make a line of scrimmage decision.

Mr. Offerman already thinks Charlotte is my long-time girlfriend, and that pleases the punch out of him. What if she was more? Go big or go home.

"Actually, Charlotte and I have just been friends since college," I say, then take a beat to deliver what he wants. "But we started dating a month ago, and we just got engaged last night. I couldn't be happier to share the news here. She's my fiancée now."

Harper drops her fork, my father blinks, and Mr. Offerman lights up. We're talking Rockefeller Christmas tree style. He's beside himself with glee over this family environment he just waltzed into. He thought he was getting a playboy, and instead he's landed a groom-to-be.

"And I would be thrilled to bring my beautiful and brilliant fiancée to your dinner tomorrow," I add, then flash my dad a big grin before I dig into my scrambled eggs. My sister is staring at me like she's about to commence a cross-examination. I'm sure she will later. But I have a busy day ahead of me now.

All I have to do is convince Charlotte that this is part of our pact.

CHAPTER FOUR

Standing on the street outside the restaurant, Dad runs his hand through his hair. His brow is furrowed. His expression is flummoxed. He just sent Mr. Offerman off to the Fifth Avenue store in a town car, letting him know he'd join him there soon.

But first he must grill me. Understandably.

"When were you going to tell me?"

Here's the thing. I can't tell him I'm faking it for Mr. Offerman.

If my dad knows that I just pulled that engagement out of my ass for the sake of his business deal, he'll think he has no choice but to apologize to Mr. Offerman. He'll walk up to him, fix on his Honest Abe look, and say he's sorry, but his son was just joking. That's the kind of man he is, and the kind of business he runs. And if he has to go back to his hand-picked buyer, tail between his legs, and confess that his party-boy son put his foot in his mouth, that'll screw up his big sale in a heartbeat.

Nope. Can't let that happen.

I won't put my dad in the position of being in on this fake engagement. But the fact is, he *needs* me to be engaged. I saw the look in Mr. Offerman's eyes when I dropped the *E* word. As Single Spencer, Man About Town, I'm the wild card in this deal that's not quite sealed. With a ring on Charlotte's finger, I become the golden child.

So I do something I don't want to do, but I have to do it.

Pad the lie. Make it airtight.

"It just happened last night, when I asked her."

"I didn't even know you were dating," he adds.

A woman in a tight pink skirt and black heels walks in our direction. She shoots me a flirty look, and I'm about to smile back when I realize I need to cut myself off.

Ouch. I've just handcuffed my favorite appendage for the next few weeks.

But that's okay. I can do this. I can pretend to be engaged. I can put my dick on ice. So to speak.

"I wanted to tell you right away, and well, 'right away' was this morning."

"How long have you been together?"

Keep it simple. Keep it short.

"It all happened so quickly, Pops," I say, adopting a look of wonderment and hopefully puppy-love for my bride-to-be. "We've always gotten along so well, as you know, and been great friends. I think it was one of those things where the one for you is just right under your nose, but we didn't realize it for the longest time. Then one night a few weeks ago, we admitted that we had feelings for each other, and…bam. The rest is history."

Wow. Did that sound believable or what? I can so do this.

Dad holds up a hand. "Not so fast. What does that mean? *The rest is history*? How did you propose? And for Christ's sake, where did you get the ring from? If you say Shane Company, I will disown you," he says in mock seriousness.

I need a ring, stat. A big-ass ring. The son of a jewelry magnate would get nothing less for his lady.

"We fell in love fast, Dad. We dated for a few weeks." That sounds plausible enough. But it would sound a *little* better like this… "That was all we needed, because it was built on the foundation of years of friendship. You know what they say. 'Marry your best friend,'" I say, though I have no clue if anyone really says that. But even so, I might as well be slamming the basketball into the net with that one, because it sounds fucking awesome. My dad nods in understanding as I finish my ode to my fictional love affair. "When you realize that you can't go a day without the woman you adore by your side, you need to make her yours, whether you've been dating a few weeks, or been in love with her for years. So I proposed last night. Couldn't wait any longer. When you just know something is right, you go for it, don't you think?"

He sighs in delight as a cab swoops along the road. "I couldn't have said it better myself."

He should hire me to write his ads. That was money.

"But no, I don't have a ring," I say, then I wink. "Would you happen to know somewhere that I could get one right away?"

He strokes his chin, pretending to be deep in thought. "Ah, I just might know the place." He laughs at his own cleverness and clasps my arm. "Come by at two, and Nina will hook you up with a beautiful stone and setting. You can't be engaged without a ring from Katharine's."

"Truer words…"

My phone buzzes in my pocket. Charlotte's ringtone— the Darth Vader entrance march. She picked it herself as a joke.

"Charlotte," I say to my dad as I gesture to the phone.

"Maybe change that now that she's going to be your wife," my dad suggests. Then he points at me, a smile on his face. "Hey! That was my first official piece of advice to you as a soon-to-be-married man."

A momentary spate of nerves lodges in my chest. What if Charlotte won't go along with the plan? What if she laughs at me—as she fucking should—and tells me this is the craziest idea in the world, and no way is she going to do it?

I tell myself not to panic prematurely. This is what friends do for each other. They pretend they're going to marry you when you need them to. Right?

The ringtone sounds again. Vader is marching closer.

"You should answer it now. Women like that," my dad says. "Hey. That's my second great piece of advice."

I steel myself, slide my thumb across the screen and go into character. "Good morning to my beautiful bride-to-be," I say in a smooth, romantic voice.

She cracks up. "Why are we playing so early? Don't tell me you started hitting the sauce on a Friday morning? Are you drunk off your ass already, Spence?"

"I'm just drunk on you. Where are you right now?"

"Just talked with one of our suppliers. Got us an even better deal, thank you very much. Nachos are on you next time. But why are you acting like a lovesick weirdo?"

"Well, *sweetheart*," I say, meeting eyes with my dad, who gives me a thumbs up as I lay it on thick for his benefit, "I'll come see you shortly, and you can tell me all about it in person."

"Okay," she says slowly. "But the deal is good, so I don't have to give you the play-by-play in person, or even on the phone. I need to go jump in the shower anyway. And no, don't say it. I'm not literally going to jump in the shower."

I laugh. "Of course. I'll be there in twenty minutes. I can't wait to see you, too."

I almost say *pookie* before I end the call, but then I'd have to relinquish my balls to the Guys' Committee. I like my balls. I'm rather attached to them.

I end the call before she can protest and then give my dad a knowing look. "The woman needs me."

My dad waggles his eyebrows. "You must heed the call." He rubs his hands together. "This is the best news ever. I couldn't be happier. I've always liked Charlotte."

And I couldn't feel any guiltier. I rarely lied to my dad as a kid. I'm pretty sure I've never done it as an adult. The morsels of guilt zipping around inside are new to me, and they're kind of crummy. But it'll be worth it. The deal memo's done; the contract will be inked in a matter of days. This little lie will help the transition go smoothly.

He grabs me in a big embrace. "Call your mother later. She'll want to hear it all from you."

"I'll give her all the mushy details," I say, wincing inside as I prep to lie to Mom as well.

I catch a cab to Charlotte's. Along the way I text Nick to cancel. *Family stuff this weekend. Gotta bail tomorrow. We'll celebrate another time?*

It'll take him hours to reply. Nick is the rare breed of modern man, sometimes spotted in the wild without a screen in his face. He's a pen and paper kind of guy, due in no small part to him being a world-class cartoonist.

As the yellow car zips along Lexington Avenue, I look up *Bang Her*, the hot bartender, then fire off a quick text: *Sorry, babe. Something came up, and I need to see the fam. Another time.*

Her reply arrives thirty seconds later. *You have an open invitation with me. :)*

Those are two of my favorite words—open invitation.

But she's not the one I'm thinking of when I arrive in Murray Hill. It's the woman behind a massive bouquet of...balloons?

CHAPTER FIVE

Easily, there are three dozen of those suckers. All the size of Martian heads, in every shade of pastel known to HGTV.

A centerpiece balloon rises in the middle, higher and prouder than the rest. That one is the lone bright shade. It's blood red, and I think it's supposed to be shaped like a heart, but it looks like a big butt to me.

I hand the cabbie a twenty, telling him to keep the change, and shut the door behind me as he screeches off in search of the next fare.

I can't even see her face. Or her chest. Or her waist. The top half of her is entirely obscured by balloons, but I'd recognize those legs anywhere. Charlotte ran track in high school, and has strong, toned legs with muscular calves that look like sin come to life when she wears high heels. Come to think of it, they're fuck-hot right now in white socks and sneakers. She must have been out for her morning run earlier today.

Peering down the street at her, I watch the scene unfold as I eat up the sidewalk with long strides. She tries to hand the bouquet to a mother pushing a stroller. The mom gives her a shake of the head and a sneer. As I cut the distance to ten feet, she offers the balloons to a girl who looks to be about ten.

"No way!" the girl shouts, and runs the other direction.

From behind the balloons, Charlotte heaves a frustrated sigh.

"Let me guess," I say as I reach her. "You've either ditched The Lucky Spot to attempt a new career as a balloon peddler, or Bradley Dipstick has struck again?"

"Third time this week. He can't seem to understand the meaning of the words 'we are never getting back together.'" She yanks the balloons away from her face, but they bat her hair. She tries again to slam them away, but static cling is working against her. The pastel fuckers are relentless, and a slight breeze keeps jamming them closer to Charlotte's hair. "These are the world's most obnoxious balloons, and I swear the other residents are whispering about his plan to get me back, since they all know about what he did in the first place."

"He just sent them, I take it?"

"Yes," she says through gritted teeth, as she clutches the bouquet. "About two minutes after I called you, I was heading out to get a quick coffee, and the doorman rang to tell me they had these balloons for me. But they were too big to fit in the elevator, so could I please come take them? Even if I wanted to keep them I wouldn't be able to get them to my apartment."

"And you're trying to give them away?" I ask as I extend a hand, gesturing for her to give them to me.

"I thought perhaps a child might enjoy them more than an adult woman. Shockingly, I've outgrown my balloon fetish."

A bus groans to a stop outside her building, and a plume of exhaust sends a balloon straight for Charlotte's face.

"Oomph," she utters, as a vile cotton candy pink balloon attacks her.

I grab the tangled mess of string and jerk it away from her, then hold them high above my head. "We can't just let them fly away into the sky? Float over Manhattan in shades of garish Easter egg?"

She shakes her head. "No. Balloons eventually lose their helium and then they float down. They get stuck on trees or fall to the ground, and animals eat them, and get sick, and that is not okay."

Charlotte is a softie. She loves animals.

"Gotcha," I say with a nod. "Just so I'm clear. Are you okay witnessing the massacre of three dozen obnoxious balloons right about now?"

She nods resolutely. "It might scar me a little bit, but I'm confident I can get through it."

"Cover your ears," I say, then grab my keys with my free hand and proceed to stab each balloon with a loud pop, including the ass-shaped one, until I'm holding a limp bouquet of broken rubber.

Sort of like Bradley.

Here's everything you need to know about how Bradley earned his stripes as a total asshole. He and Charlotte met two years ago since they both lived in the same building. They started dating, hitting it off and going strong for a while. They talked about moving in together. They decided to buy a bigger place on the tenth floor and get engaged. Everything was going swimmingly until the day they were all set to sign the papers on the two-bedroom, and Bradley headed down early to—get this—"check out the pipes." Yeah, that was his real excuse.

When Charlotte arrived, pen in hand, Bradley was banging the realtor against the kitchen counter.

"I never did care for those steel counters," Charlotte had said, and I'd been so proud of her for coming up with that zinger in the heat of the moment.

Of course, in reality, she'd been devastated. She'd loved the guy. She'd cried on my shoulder as she told me the story, zinger and all. That had been ten months ago, and when Bradley finally ditched the realtor, he embarked on a campaign to win Charlotte back.

With gifts.

Abhorrent gifts.

I stuff the flaccid balloons into the garbage can on the corner. "The animals are safe now from his reign of terror."

"Thank you," she says with relief, as she grabs a tie from her wrist and yanks her hair off her face and into a quick ponytail. "That was like a pastel explosion of pathetic. Once you killed them, they were pretty droopy, too."

"Like Bradley?" I ask with an arch of the eyebrow.

Her lips quirk into a tiny grin. She's trying not to laugh. She covers her mouth. Charlotte has never been one to kiss and tell. She never shared details of their sex life—not that I wanted to know any. But she was a vault.

So the fact that she's holding up a thumb and forefinger, and mouthing *a little bit* is a huge deal for her.

For me too, it turns out.

I'm a guy, and therefore I'm in competition with all men, all the time, so I can't help but feel a surge of triumph.

That is so not an issue for me whatsoever.

"Let's get you that coffee and I'll tell you why I was acting like a lovesick weirdo."

CHAPTER SIX

As she pours sugar into her cup, her eyes widen. As she adds a drop of half and half, they turn into saucers. And as she brings the coffee to her lips, her eyeballs practically pop out of her head.

When I mention the dinner tomorrow, she nearly spits out the hot beverage.

Then she clutches her belly, clasps her hand on her mouth, and shudders with laughter. "How do you get yourself into these situations?"

"I like to think it's my wit and charm, but in this case, it might have been my big mouth," I say, with a *what can you do?* shrug. Thing is, there's only one answer to that question—I have to show up with a fiancée. Which means *she* has to say yes, so I turn serious. "Will you do it? Will you pretend to be engaged to me for a week?"

The laughter doesn't stop. "That's your brilliant idea? That's your best solution to the foot-in-the-mouth problem?"

"Yes," I say, nodding, staying firm to the plan. "It's a great idea."

"Oh, Spencer. That's fantastic. Really, truly, one of your best ideas ever." She leans against the creamer counter at this hip little coffee shop near her place. "And by 'best idea,' I mean 'worst.'"

"Why? Tell me, why is it such a bad idea?"

She takes a deliberate pause, then holds one finger in the air for emphasis and speaks. "Correct me if I'm wrong, but you *want* this fake engagement to work, right? You want to pull it off?"

"Yes. Obviously."

She stabs her finger against her sternum. "And so your bright idea is to ask me?"

"Who else would I ask?"

She rolls her eyes. "You're aware that I'm pretty much the worst liar in the universe?"

"I wouldn't call you the worst."

She stares at me like I'm crazy. I think I might be. "Do I need to remind you of the time in junior year when you and your friends pranked my dorm? If memory serves, I not only witnessed your prank, thanks to skipping out of *The Notebook* screening early, but my roomies got the truth about whodunit in about five seconds."

"You couldn't have caved that quickly," I insist, taking a drink of my coffee as I flash back to college. One of my buddies had been dating one of Charlotte's friends. The girlfriend had hung his TV remote from a fourth-story window, since she thought he watched too much TV, and to get even he enlisted a bunch of us in a little furniture switcheroo. Trouble was, Charlotte caught us in the act, so I swore her to secrecy, promising we'd return everything after midnight.

"Oh, I did. I absolutely did. It wasn't hard to get the truth out of me," she says adamantly, looking me straight in the eyes. "All they had to do was ask who relocated all the common room furniture to the laundry room, then tickle it out of me. If I could have made it through that movie I never would have walked in on the prank. I still blame Nicholas Sparks for my failure to protect your trick."

"I promise you won't be forced to sit through a Nicholas Sparks film under this fake engagement scenario. And I swear there won't be any tickle torture confessions."

"Look, I just think this is not only ridiculous, but also highly likely to blow up in your face." She softens her tone. "I care about you, Spencer. I know you want to make this pretend engagement work for your dad's sake, but of all the women you know in New York, why on earth would you pick me? Even an escort agency would be smarter. Those women know how to be believable fiancée types."

I scoff at the idea and then clasp my hand on her shoulder, squeezing her, like a coach trying to persuade a free agent to join his team. I need to convince her she can do this. Because she can. She knows me better than anyone. Plus, I can't just call up an escort agency and order up a fiancée for a week. *"Hello, can I have the full girlfriend experience with a side of fries to go, please?"* One, I don't know any escort agencies. Two, the buck stops at Charlotte. I offered her up this morning as my bride. It's Charlotte or nothing.

"It won't even take up that much time. It'll just be a few events to go to together—picking out a ring today, then this dinner thing tomorrow. You can do this. It's you and me, babe," I say, and she furrows her brow at the last word.

"Is that what you call me as your fiancée? Babe? Or is it sweetheart? Or something else? Snookums? Honey bear? Sweet cheeks? Snuffaluffagus?"

"I assure you, it's not Snuffaluffagus."

"I kind of like Snuffaluffagus," she says, and now she's just trying to pull my leg...or maybe avoid giving me an answer.

"I guess it's babe then," I say, staying the course, as she drinks some of her coffee. "I don't know why I called you that. Except for the obvious. You're a babe."

She smiles again and says in the softest voice, "Thank you. So are you."

See? Charlotte and I can both appreciate each other's appearance. That's one of the great hallmarks of our friendship. I can acknowledge she is a babe, and she can do the same with me, and we're still all good. That's why she *has* to be my pretend fiancée.

I gesture from her to me, confidence coursing through me. Maybe it's a false bravado. Maybe it's real. But it's all I've got, and I need her. The clock's ticking on the two p.m. opening curtain at Katharine's. "My point is this. We've done this. It's our game," I say, like I'm convincing her to join the crew I'm assembling for a Vegas casino heist. "We know the drill. I play fake fiancé with you all the time, and you with me."

She worries away at the corner of her lip. It's kind of ridiculously cute. Like, if she were really my fiancée, I'd probably think that was adorable, and I would lean in for a quick peck.

"That's for three minutes, at the most, at a bar," she points out. "That's just a quick wham bam, thank you, ma'am kind of thing to save each other from unwanted advances. For this I'd have to keep it up for a week, you're saying? Under scrutiny? Of the press, your parents, your dad's buyer, and everyone else? I just think you're asking for trouble."

"Yes, but who knows me better than you? You're the only person who could possibly pull this off," I say, and as a new rush of customers streams into the tiny coffee shop, we head out, making our way back toward her building, coffee cups in hand as we walk.

"I want to help you. You know I do. I just think everyone will know we're not really engaged, and then that's not helpful to you at all."

Undeterred, I press on. "Then let's have a debrief. Especially since I'm supposed to buy you a ring at two p.m." Her eyes go wide, and I keep reassuring her. "Let's go over every single thing we need to know."

"Like what toothpaste I use, and whether you hog the sheets?"

"I don't hog the sheets," I say as we sidestep a husband and wife, each wearing babies in Björns and arguing about where to brunch.

"And I use minty-fresh Crest. The teeth-whitening kind," she says. "But let's be honest. That's not what anyone is going to ask. Also, have you thought about how you're going to survive a week or more without your favorite pastime?" she says, as an evil glint lights up her brown eyes.

"I can handle being celibate."

She nods. "Sure. Keep telling that to yourself." She stops and points at me. "But I'm serious—if I do this, you better not mess around with anyone else after hours."

Hope bounces wildly in my chest. "Does that mean you're saying yes?"

She shakes her head. "Not yet. I'm just pointing out another potential roadblock for you. It's going to be a loooong seven days for you," she says, elbowing me in the ribs. "Besides, how are you going to manage the fact that you were basically publicly dating a few weeks ago? What are you going to tell your dad and his buyer about that? Or how about the woman you saw in Miami a month ago at the restaurant opening?"

I wave a hand like the escape artist I am. "Leave it to the master. If anything comes up about that celebrity trainer, I'll just deny it. No one believes the gossip rags anyway. And the Miami thing was just a friendly, posed photo. Besides, I already devised a perfect story of how we fell in love. I told my dad it happened quickly. In just a few weeks, in fact, and that I proposed to you last night because I realized after all these years that I'd been in love with you the whole time."

"The whole time?" she asks, lifting an eyebrow.

I shrug playfully. "The whole damn time. I've been head over heels. It finally dawned on me what I was feeling, and I got down on one knee to make you mine."

She doesn't say anything at first, just parts her lips, and I stare at them for longer than usual. They are really pretty lips. I mean, from an empirical point of view. As her fake fiancé, it's good for me to be knowledgeable about all her features, including her lips.

Assuming she says yes. She has to say yes.

"That's actually a sweet story," she says, her voice completely sincere as we stand on the corner of her block, holding each other's gaze. "A true friends-to-lovers romance?"

"Yes," I say quickly, breaking the eye contact because it's a bit too much for me to handle right now. I have no clue why it feels weird, whether it's the words or the way she looks at me.

Or really, *why* I feel weird at all.

We keep walking, and she takes a hearty gulp of her coffee. She straightens her spine and draws in a breath, and I cross my fingers that she's about to agree.

"I want to help you, but…" she says, her voice trailing off.

My chest craters. Like, worse than those deflated balloons. I am out of air. I'm going to have to tell my dad the engagement ended before it even started, hang my head, cry in my soup, and claim Charlotte dumped me and broke my heart.

"Crap," she mutters. "*Incoming douche.*"

It's the total asshole himself. Bradley "Bend Her Over The Counter" Buckingham walks toward us. He hates me. Not that I give a shit, but he detests me because I had the audacity to advise Charlotte against buying an apartment with him. It didn't make financial sense to go in together in this building when other residences in the hood were increasing in value faster.

He's about six feet, which makes him two inches shorter than me. He has blondish-red hair, broad shoulders, and the cheesy grin of a vacuum cleaner salesman. He works in PR. He's senior VP of Communications for a huge pharmaceutical company that's always under fire. King of Spin. Ace of Liars. Captain of Scum.

"Charlotte!" he calls out, waving to her. "Did you get the balloons?"

He pulls up next to us, barely making eye contact with me.

"They didn't fit in the elevator, but it really doesn't matter. You need to stop sending me gifts. It's over with us. In fact," she says, and reaches out to grab my free hand, threading her fingers through mine and surprising the fuck out of me, since she's not a hand-holder, "I'm engaged to Spencer now."

Whoa.

That surprise over her holding my hand? It's nothing compared to the surprise from what comes next.

She thrusts her coffee cup at Bradley, and in the blink of an eye she wraps her hands around my neck, and presses her lips to mine.

CHAPTER SEVEN

Charlotte is kissing me.

On the streets of New York.

Her lips are on mine.

She tastes fantastic.

Like cream and sugar and coffee and sweetness. Like all the good things in the world. Like I imagined she'd taste.

Not that I've been thinking about kissing my best friend.

But, look, you can't help where your mind wanders sometimes as a guy. Any man who is friends with a woman has taken the old imagination out for a stroll to Kissing Avenue, then Lovers Lane, then Fucking Street.

Which is exactly what I'm going to be visiting in Ye Olde Brain if she keeps brushing those lips softly against mine in this fluttery, lingering kind of kiss. Because it is getting harder to think about anything other than turning up the volume on this lip-lock.

A lot harder.

She lets out the tiniest little noise—like a sigh, or a gasp, or an almost-but-not-quite moan. And if she does that again, I will be pushing her against the slate-gray brick wall of her building, caging her in, sliding my hands along her sides and turning this into a full-body kiss.

Because she is too fucking sexy for her own good.

For *my* good.

She lets go of my lips.

My hard-on doesn't get the message to chill out. It's still pointing in her direction, wanting more. I cycle to my certified best buzzkill, picturing sweaty basketball players, and it goes down as Charlotte flashes a devilishly satisfied grin at Bradley.

While Charlotte was busy devouring me on Lexington Avenue, Bradley's jaw had become dislodged from his face and fell to the ground.

Excellent.

"We got engaged last night. And I couldn't be happier," she says, snuggling up next to me and snaking an arm around my waist.

He tries to speak, but fish air bubbles come out instead.

Oh, this is priceless. I stare down at my shoes. I'm not smirking right now. I swear I haven't got a big-ass grin on my face. I'm just the innocent bystander who got lip-smacked by the goddess.

"And like I said, it would be *awesome* if you could stop assaulting me with balloons and teddy bears and chocolate-covered cherries," she says, and I make a quiet snort. Charlotte can't stand chocolate-covered cherries. How does he not know this?

"I don't even like them," she says to Bradley, as she inches her fingers tighter around my waist. So tight that for a sliver of a second it seems like...like she's copping a feel of my abs.

Okay.

That's not even remotely a problem at all. *Those rock-solid abs are there for your pleasure, m'lady.*

"I had no idea you two were involved," Bradley says. I look up to see the wheels turning in his head. "Were you always?"

Charlotte's expression morphs into one of complete, slack-jawed shock. "What did you just say?"

He's graduated. I didn't think it was possible. But he just earned the title of Master Asshole.

Time to step in.

"No, Bradley. It's all new. It's all quite recent," I say, meeting his eyes. "And to be honest, I really owe you a huge debt of thanks. If it wasn't for you, and those quality control tests you performed on the kitchen counter, we might never have had the chance to be together. So thank you for fucking up a good thing with the most amazing woman in the world. 'Cause now she's mine." Then to bust his chops one more time, I drag her against me caveman-style, bend her backward, and kiss her hard again.

In seconds, I pull her up, wave good-bye to her ex, and guide her into her building.

I'm not sure if she's more shocked by what he just said, what I just did, or by her own spur-of-the-moment decision, but as soon as we're in the elevator, she turns to me, and shrugs happily. "I guess I'm playing your fiancée for the next week, Snuffaluffagus. We've got to buy a ring at two, and I'm going to require a full debrief."

There are other things I'd like to debrief right now. But this works too.

* * *

I do my best work in the bedroom. This is completely my domain. So it should be no big deal that she asked me to wait here. But something about being in Charlotte's bedroom is wigging me out.

Mostly because there's nudity transpiring mere feet away.

She's taking a shower, and no matter how you slice them, New York apartments are thimble size. Let me spell this out—There is a wet, naked, hot woman in a ten-foot radius.

Got it? Okay. Moving on.

I pick up a picture frame on her sky blue bureau, a photo of the dog her parents have. A fluffy brown summa dog—some of this, some of that. I'm going to focus on this mutt. Zero in on him. Look at his tail. Check out his ears. Yup, this picture is doing the trick. It is helping me not to linger on the naked woman and how well she kisses.

Or how much I liked it.

Why the fuck did I like it so much?

Of course you liked it, idiot. You're a straight male and a pretty woman kisses you—you'd be stupid not to like it. End of story. Doesn't mean anything. Stop analyzing.

Especially since she just turned off the shower.

Maybe she forgot a towel. Maybe she'll open the door a crack, and ask me to grab one for her.

I smack my forehead. *Get it together, Holiday.*

I set down the picture, inhale deeply, and straighten my shoulders. The door creaks open. She steps out of the bathroom wearing only a white fluffy towel wrapped above her breasts.

"You might be wondering why I asked you to wait in my bedroom instead of the living room," she says, in the most matter-of-fact of tones.

I have no clue how she can be talking like we're having a business transaction while droplets of water slide down her bare legs. But I'm a strong man. I can handle this. I'm not tempted at all by my best friend. My dick, however, begs to differ, the traitorous prick.

"The thought crossed my mind," I say, as I lean against the bureau, striking a casual pose.

"Because if you're my fiancé, you need to be comfortable with me being naked," she says with a crisp nod.

Shit, she's going to do it. She's going to drop the towel. She's going to make us practice fucking. I am the luckiest man on the face of the earth.

Wait. No. I can't fuck my best friend. I absolutely, positively, can't screw Charlotte. Even if she tosses the towel on the floor and begs me to.

I lace my fingers together behind my back, linking my twitchy hands.

"Okay, so you're getting naked," I say, doing my best to imitate her cool-as-a-cucumber tone, which is throwing me off big time.

"No. It's the *idea* of me naked," she corrects.

I give her a pointed look. "Seems to me it's both the idea and the reality."

"Fine, fine. They're one and the same, and it's part of the debrief."

"Is this the exam portion?"

She walks past me, her arm brushing against mine before she yanks open the top drawer of the bureau. "Yes. This is more like the practical lab instruction."

"And this is because you somehow think we're going to be required to be naked together in front of Mr. Offerman in order to pull this off? This isn't like some reality show fake engagement where we have to pass certain skills in an obstacle course. You know that, right?"

She nods as she hunts around in the drawer. "I'm aware of that. I see this as more like the Newlywed Game."

"And in this version we're quizzed on how accustomed I am to the idea of you naked and vice versa?"

Her breath hitches when I say that—*vice versa.*

I don't know what to make of that small gasp...like if it means something about the idea of me *au naturel.*

She spins around and holds up two pairs of panties, one in each hand. "Quick. Do you prefer it when your fiancée wears the black lace thong?" She waggles a scrap of silky-looking fabric that is so hot my face might be engulfed in flames right now because Charlotte owns *that?* "Or do you prefer her in the white side-string bikini?" She waves the white pair before my eyes, and all I can see is a tiny triangular patch of fabric that's the slightest bit see-through.

Forget the flames. I am a fucking inferno right now knowing she owns *this* too. White panties that reveal pretty much everything.

Lord have mercy.

If a woman I was dating wore those panties, they wouldn't be on her. They'd be in my teeth as I pulled them off. I can't do anything but stare at her lingerie as my blood heats to surface-of-Mercury levels.

Charlotte tilts her head and shoots me an expectant look. "Which one do you prefer your fiancée in?"

I haven't answered her yet. I'm just trying to get the blood flowing from other parts of my anatomy back to my brain.

"Nothing," I say, intending it as a jokey retort, but my throat is dry and scratchy, so the words come out in a harsh growl.

She lifts an eyebrow, completely unperturbed. "Nothing? Really? Okay then," she says, and swivels around, stuffing the underthings back in the bureau, grabbing a bra, then closing the drawer with a gentle ping. "That makes things easier. I'll be right back."

She touches my shoulder playfully with her index finger, yanks open her closet, grabs something from a hanger, and returns to the bathroom. As she shuts the door, I sink down on the bed and breathe out hard. I drop my forehead to my palm. What the hell kind of test was that? That was a feat of strength, if I ever experienced one.

But I don't have time to figure it out because twenty seconds later, she opens the bathroom door and says, "What do you think?"

She's wearing a cranberry red skirt that falls to her knees and kind of flares out as she twirls around, along with a black silky tank. "Does this work for you to take me ring shopping?"

I point at her midsection, then lower. "You're really not wearing underwear?"

Her eyes sparkle with mischief. "My fiancé told me he prefers me in..." She steps closer, drops a hand to my shoulder, and brings her lips to my ear to whisper, "Nothing."

And now, ladies and gentlemen, my cock is officially saluting my best friend, the Commando Temptress. She pops back into her closet, emerges with a pair of black heels, and slips them on.

Kill me now.

Her legs look insanely hot, and knowing that the treasure at the apex of her thighs is bare is going to drive me crazy. I drag both hands through my hair like bulldozers. "Okay, you win the first feat of strength." I march over to her bureau where I open the top drawer, grab the bikini underwear and wave it like a white flag. "I'm surrendering."

She furrows her brow. "That's all it takes for you to bow out? I thought you wanted and needed me to be your fiancée?"

"I do. I absolutely do. But you cannot go out without underwear on. You cannot waltz around New York stark naked under that skirt. Put these on," I say, thrusting them at her.

Her lips quirk up in a grin. The corners seem to twitch back and forth. I swear her eyes say *I told you so*.

I hold my hands out wide. "Okay, Cheshire Cat. What canary did you eat?"

She takes the panties in her hand, grabs my arm, and tugs me into the bathroom. She points at the mirror. There's a note on it, written in red lipstick. *Spencer will make me put on the white bikinis.*

And I crack up—deep, big chuckles that come from the very heart of me. I point a finger at her. "And you said you weren't a good liar."

She drops her jaw, then places her hand on her chest. "I wasn't lying. That's the truth, written in red lipstick two minutes ago, and I was right. Admit it."

"You were playing me."

"No. I was *proving* to myself that I could pull off being your fiancée," she says with a wicked grin, bumping me with her hip. The look in her eyes is a cocktail mix of pride and amusement. "I wanted to see if we knew each other well." She pauses before she says the next thing, lowering her voice. "And intimately."

Then she steps into the panties.

In front of me.

With her heels on.

Over one ankle, then the other, then she slides them seductively up her smooth, strong legs. My eyes track her the whole time. I couldn't look away if I tried, and I'm beginning to accept that I'm just gonna be sporting wood even more than usual during this next week. I figure that's normal, right? What red-blooded man could be in close proximity to a gorgeous woman who's putting on a pair of see-through—

My brain stops processing words. I swallow dryly.

The panties are over her knees. They're gliding up her thighs. Making their way to her bare—

"Close your eyes," she whispers.

And because I'm a gentleman, I do. I see black and silvery stars behind my lids, but I'm picturing everything I'm missing right now. Yup. Round-the-clock pocket rocket. Just resign myself to perpetual wood. Can't fight these things. No need to even try.

"You can open them," she says, and I oblige. She points to the toilet seat. "Take a seat, partner. Let's debrief as I do my hair and makeup."

CHAPTER EIGHT

We review the vitals.

She's a sheet-hogger. I sleep naked. She doesn't like sharing the bathroom sink at the same time. I couldn't care less if she spits out toothpaste while I'm brushing. She has more than two dozen different lotions from The Body Shop and wears a different one each day of the week.

"Obviously, I don't use lotion," I say, gesturing to the silver bathroom cart full of orange blossom, honey vanilla, coconut island, and every other flavor of body rub under the sun. "And again, I don't think anyone will be quizzing us on whether I know what kind of lotion you wear."

"I know that," she says as she plugs in a hair dryer. "But the point is, *I* want to feel like we know these things about each other so it will be believable that we'd be engaged. For instance, it takes me five minutes to dry my hair."

I set the stopwatch on my phone and read a chapter in a thriller as she blows out her hair. Something about this moment feels very domestic. Like we really are a couple, and I'm waiting for my woman to get ready to go out.

Hmmm.

Maybe because that's precisely what's happening.

Except the part about us being a real couple.

When the buzzer sounds, she's done, so I put my phone in my pocket. After she winds up the dryer cord, she snaps her fingers. "We forgot one very important thing."

"What's that?"

"How did we know?"

"How did we know what?"

"Duh. That we were in love." She says it so sweetly, so convincingly, that for a second my mind goes blank. I forget we're rehearsing, and I simply stretch back in time and try to pinpoint. Then the reality smacks me, and I laugh to myself. We're not in love. We're playing pretend. So as we leave her bathroom, I tell her what I told my dad this morning about how we came together.

"That's not enough," she says, her heels clicking on the hardwood floor as we cross the short distance to her sliver of a kitchen.

"Why not?" I ask, as she grabs a cold pitcher of iced tea from the fridge and I take two glasses from the cupboard. She's particular about her iced tea. Makes it herself with these tea bags from Peets that she orders on Amazon, since Peets isn't in New York.

"We need more details," she says as she takes a drink. "I bet Mr. Offerman's daughters will be the first to sniff out a lie. Girls are smart like that, and if his daughters catch on, you bet they're telling Daddy. We need this solid. So, it was one night at the bar when we supposedly realized we had it bad for each other, right?"

"Yes. Just a few weeks ago. It all happened quickly."

"But how did it start? Specifically? What was that one thing that started our romance?"

"Charlotte, it was my dad I told the story to. He didn't ask."

"But women will," she points out, then wiggles her bare fingers. "Once I've got that ring on, all the women will be cooing over it and asking for the details of how we fell in love. Probably tomorrow at dinner. We need a story," she says emphatically as she paces in the small kitchen. Then her eyes light up with excitement. "I got it! One Thursday night at The Lucky Spot, over a glass of wine after closing time, you made a joke about how everyone thinks we're a couple, and I said 'maybe we should be one.' And then there was an *awkward pause* in the conversation," she says, her tone softening, as if she's reminiscing about that fateful night.

I go next, picking up the Mad Libs thread of our make-believe love story. "Only it wasn't awkward. It was simply right," I say, shooting her my best love-struck smile. "And we admitted then that we had feelings for each other."

"And we had the hottest kiss ever. Obviously."

I scoff. "Not just the hottest kiss. We had the hottest sex ever," I say, because I *have* to up the ante like that.

She blushes, stays silent, and finishes her iced tea. I take another drink of mine and then place both glasses in her dishwasher, lining them up neatly on the top row, just like she prefers.

"Then to keep it simple, let's pretend you proposed to me at the bar last night, since that's where it all started. You proposed after everyone left. You got down on one knee and said you couldn't even wait to get me a ring, but I had to be yours."

"Perfect. Love it. Easy to remember."

I close the dishwasher, and she meets my gaze. Her brown eyes are soft and sweet. "Spencer. Thank you."

I give her a look like she's crazy. "For putting the glasses in the dishwasher?"

"No. For putting up with all that." She waves in the general direction of the rest of her apartment. "I was kind of putting you through your paces now. But I needed to feel like we could pull this off."

"Do you now? Do you feel like you're on your way to becoming Mrs. Holiday?"

She laughs. "That's funny. Those are two words that we'll never hear together again," she says, running her hand absently down my arm as we leave the kitchen. "You're the avowed bachelor for life."

I nod, confirming my status. Total playboy. One hundred percent swinging single. No need to lasso this free bird. "Absolutely."

She reaches for her purse on her living room table. "Wait. There's just one more test."

"You're going to make me jump through another hoop? Sheesh. You are a pistol."

She huffs. "I hardly think selecting my panties is some Herculean task. But be that as it may, this test is for me. It's the final test to make sure I'm ready to walk into your dad's store in our first public appearance as Mr. Holiday and his bride-to-be."

I cross my arms, waiting to see what she'll do next.

She looks me right in the eye, her lips a straight line, her expression starkly serious. "I need you to try to tickle the truth out of me."

I arch an eyebrow skeptically. "For real?"

She nods. "Absolutely. You know it's my weakness," she says, backing up to her soft gray couch, and flopping down amidst a sea of pillows in blues, reds, and purples. She loves jewel-toned colors. As she lies across the cushions, the golden blonde strands of her hair fan out over a royal blue pillow. "Do it," she commands. "I need to know I won't cave. I need to prove to myself that even the torture of tickling won't make me give up the secrets of my best friend."

I unbutton my cuffs and roll up my shirt sleeves to my forearms.

"Don't go easy on me," she says.

"Not in my nature."

"Make me squirm. Make it pure torture. Make me want to give it up. That's the only way we'll know if I can truly handle this charade for the next week."

I hold my hands out wide. "All I can say, Snuffaluffagus, is you're on."

I run the few feet to the couch and go for it. I am a ferocious tickler and a tenacious competitor, and even though this is Charlotte, I'm not going to let up. Diving in, I tickle her waist, and in a nanosecond, she is wiggling.

"Admit it—you're not really engaged to Spencer Holiday," I say, like a harsh cross-examiner.

"He's going to be my hubby, I swear," she shrieks as I tickle harder, digging in.

"I don't believe you. Tell the truth. It's all an act. He made you do it."

She squeals as she thrashes back and forth in a wild attempt to scramble away from me. Her uncontrollable laughter ripples through her. "I've been crazy about him forever."

"I don't believe you," I bark, as I grapple with her hips. She might as well be an eel, she's fighting so hard to wiggle away. She practically burrows into the couch pillows to escape my tickling. But I'm strong, and I've got her pinned. I move up her sides, and she arches her entire back in a curve.

"Oh my God, no!"

Holy shit. She is beyond ticklish. This is epic ticklishness. Her face is all scrunched up, her nose is crinkled, and her mouth is wide open as she laughs ceaselessly.

"Why? Why are you crazy about him?" I demand as I try to break her down with rib tickles. In a knee-jerk reaction, she literally does just that—jams her knee into my stomach to try to make me stop. I block it, and her kneecap grazes my hip. Doesn't even hurt.

"Because," she says on a breathless pant, as my fingers race up her sides, "he makes me laugh."

I'm near her armpits now. "Why else?"

"Because he opens the door for me," she says, hitting a high note on the last word as I reach her most ticklish spot.

"One more reason," I demand as I trap her, my lower body pinning her, and I capture one leg between both of mine.

Her laughter ceases abruptly, and her eyes widen. "He's huge," she says in a whisper.

We both go silent for a few seconds. Then I nod approvingly and end the torment. "You have proven your loyalty to the cause."

I look down at her. Her hair falls in a wild mess, her black tank rides up her stomach, revealing inches of soft flesh, and her breath comes in heavy pants. This is the moment when I should move off her. I really should. She's not wiggling anymore. She's not fighting me. I'm supposed to let go, offer her a hand, and take her ring shopping.

But her eyes seem different. I've never seen them like this. Something vulnerable flickers through them. "We should practice," she says in a soft voice, her words landing on the air like snowflakes.

"Practice?" I repeat, because though I'm pretty confident what she means, I don't want to assume anything.

Her lips part, and her tongue slides across the bottom one. "What we did on the street. So it's believable."

"Is kissing part of the charade?"

She nods. "I can't imagine two people who just got en-gaged wouldn't kiss at least once tomorrow at the dinner event. It would make it more believable, don't you think? Can't look like the first time we've done it."

"Right. Like in the movies where a man and woman have to share a hotel room at some inn, and they pretend to be together, and the innkeeper says at dinner, 'Kiss the girl.' That's what you mean, right?"

She smiles beneath me, then she bites the corner of her lip like she did at the coffee shop. At the time, I resisted the impulse to give her a quick peck. Now, I don't. I press my lips to that corner and kiss her.

A soft kiss.

I pull back. Her chest rises and falls. Her eyes look wild. "Is that what you want?"

"No," she says.

"What do you want?"

"A real kiss. I want to know how my fiancé kisses for real. Not just a soft little kiss on the street."

"A real kiss. Are you sure?"

"Yes. Why wouldn't I be sure? You're not a horrid kisser, are you?" Her hand flies to her mouth. "Oh my God. That's it. You kiss in some weird way," she says as she takes her hand off her mouth.

"That just earned you serious proof of the opposite. Because I promise you, I will kiss you in the only way you should be kissed."

"What way is that?"

I gaze into her eyes, move my hips against her thigh so she can feel more of me, then say, "A real kiss should get you wet."

She gasps, and I dip my mouth to hers and kiss the sound away.

She led our first kiss. She caught me off guard on the street with a fantastic ambush, but this kiss is mine.

I control it. I lead it. And I want to tease her. To make her squirm again, only this time with desire. This time she'll be writhing to get closer to me, not to escape. I slide my tongue across her lips, and she opens them, inviting me to kiss her deeper. I don't heed her wishes. Instead, I move to her jawline, kissing her there, along her soft skin, and up to her ear. Her skin tastes amazing, like sunshine and cherries, and maybe that's the lotion she put on a few minutes ago, or maybe it's just her natural scent. Either way, it drives me crazy. My bones hum with desire as I travel to the shell of her ear. I flick my tongue against her earlobe, and she moans.

"Ohhhh."

It's not the sound she made on the street. It's louder. It's freer. It's unleashed.

And I fucking love it.

She pushes her hips up against me, trying to get closer.

I steal a glance at her closed eyes, the flush in her cheeks, the redness in her lips. She's the piece of chocolate cake in front of me that I must consume. All of it. Now. Every bite.

I rope my hands in her hair, the blonde strands spilling over my fingers in a golden tumble. With all this fantastic hair in my hands, I'm compelled to tug it. When I do, she draws a sharp breath that turns into a soft moan. My fingers curl around her skull, and I grip her head tightly, holding her in place.

Returning to her mouth, I stop teasing.

Instead, I turn it up.

Crank the volume.

Kiss her hard.

Devour her.

Our tongues tangle, our teeth click, and I swear she's melting under me, beneath me, into me. My veins thrum with lust, my cock is steel in my pants, and my brain is zeroed in on one thing—a kiss that makes her wet.

It takes all my resistance not to run my hand up her thigh, under her skirt, and across the panel of those white see-through bikini panties. But I don't have to touch her to verify she's turned on beyond any and all reason. I know in the little murmurs she makes, in the way her arms slink around my neck, in how her fingers curl into the ends of my hair. Most of all, the confirmation comes in the way she tries to rock into me. Her hips shift, move, seeking me out, and briefly my restraint snaps.

I move quickly, wedging myself between her thighs, thrusting once against her. A sexy cry escapes her lips. Her hands fly to my ass. The restraint breaks once more as she parts her legs for me, making room, inviting me to dry hump her on the couch.

Oh hell, do I want to RSVP to this offer. If I do, in a few more seconds her legs will be wrapped around my hips, and I'll want to be fucking her. Friends or strangers, how could I not want to fuck her? She's hot, she's ready, and she's raring to go.

I want to tug off those panties, sink into her heat.

But she's my best friend, and I can't do that.

Somehow, my common sense grabs the steering wheel, wresting control from my dick.

I break the kiss and jump away from her, standing in seconds. I need air. I need space. If I stay a second longer I'll push the both of us too far, and I don't want her to know the battle that just waged in my head. I give my best casual shrug, then say, "I don't even have to ask if that got you wet."

She blinks.

She scoffs.

She sits up and straightens her spine, squaring her shoulders. "I bet you'd like to know, cocky bastard," she says, as she smooths out her shirt, adjusting it, then her skirt.

The moment is awkward. We were on the precipice of dry humping, but now we're tossing zingers, and I'm still aroused to painful levels. This can't happen again. We've conducted the test; she won't feel uncomfortable pretending to be with me, and that's all there is to it. Onward and upward, and the show must go on.

A family show. Not fucking porn.

She gets up and slips around the corner into her bedroom, and I use the break to adjust myself, take a deep breath, and imagine a locker room full of hairy men.

Fuck, I want to gag.

But it works. My erection fades away.

She returns, and when she bends over to grab her purse, I can't help but notice she's wearing the black lace thong now.

I look away so the grin on my face doesn't reveal my complete cocky bastard-dom.

CHAPTER NINE

"So how about those Mets?"

As the elevator doors spread open on her floor, I guide the conservation away from that practice session on her couch. The *final* practice session. No more kissing rehearsals. Too dangerous.

"They're having a good season," she says as she yanks her purse strap higher on her shoulder, not entirely taking the bait.

"Good pitching will do that for you," I say, pressing the button for the lobby and wondering when was the last time that we talked about baseball to cover up an uncomfortable moment. She's a hard-core fan, due in no small part to the fact that she regularly crushes it in her fantasy baseball league. I've often told her if our bars fizzle, she should be a general manager, but she just laughs and tells me baseball is her love so she wants to keep it pure.

Right now, it's not pure. It's a goddamn metaphor for a true awkward moment. "Are you still killing it with your lineup?"

She turns to me, her brown eyes intensely serious. "I meant it earlier when I said no dating this week. I need to know that you're okay with that. Not even after hours."

And we're done with the baseball bullshit.

"Of course," I say quickly, tugging on my tie and acting offended. "I can't believe you think I can't manage a week without sex."

She shakes her head as the elevator chugs down. "This might seem silly to you, since this is a pretend relationship, but after what happened with Bradley..."

"Charlotte, I swear. I'm on the wagon for the next week," I say, holding up three fingers. "Scout's honor."

"You were never a boy scout."

"True. But I also don't cheat, whether I'm in a fake relationship or a real one."

She arches an eyebrow. "Have you ever been in a real one?"

"Sure. And by real, you mean the type of relationship where I know her last name, right?" I say, deadpan.

She crosses her arms. "Let me amend that. Have you ever been in a relationship that lasted longer than a fortnight?"

I make a snooty sound. "Fortnight. Aren't you fancy?"

"And Amanda from college doesn't count."

"Why not? I went out with her for four months. But yes. I have," I say, though I'm pretty damn sure I haven't. But my ability to sustain a long-term commitment isn't the point of this conversation. The point is whether my dick practices serial monogamy. "And I'll keep it in my pants for the next week, like I said I would. While we're at it, the same goes for you."

"You don't even have to worry about that."

"You mean this isn't going to cramp your style?" I ask, as the elevator slows at the lobby.

She scoffs. "Like that's possible."

"No hot dates on the agenda for the next week?"

She raises her hands and lifts all ten fingers. "It's been ten months for me," she says sharply as the doors whoosh open.

We walk across the lobby and onto Lexington, where the Uber car I ordered is waiting. I open the door for her, and she slides across. I follow her, and we buckle in. Things feel normal again between us, like we've slid out of the tunnel of awkward, and it's now just us.

"Ten months without a relationship, you mean?" I ask, since I know she hasn't been involved with anyone since the split. But come to think of it, she hasn't mentioned any dates either. Even though she doesn't kiss and tell, she still probably would have said something if she'd had a good date.

She shakes her head. "No relationship. No dates. No kissing. Nothing."

Ten months without sex. That's like a lifetime. Not sure I've gone more than ten days. Maybe fourteen tops, but that was a rough two weeks. She must be working her toys hard.

Ah, fuck. Now, I'm picturing Charlotte in bed with a purple vibrating rabbit, legs spread, hand working the ten-speed controller, breath coming fast.

Thanks, brain, for putting that fantastic image in my head to derail any intelligent thought.

Some days I wonder how men get anything accomplished at all with sex on the brain constantly. In fact, I wonder how men have ever gotten a single thing done across the whole vast expanse of time. It's a miracle we manage to tie our shoes and comb our hair.

Then it hits me. That kiss on her couch. That kiss on the street. Those were the first kisses she's had in nearly a year. *My* kisses. It makes me kind of happy that I'm the first guy she's kissed in a long time. Even though it makes no sense that I'd be glad about that. It also doesn't make sense that a dose of possessiveness over Charlotte courses through me, too. I don't want anyone else to kiss her.

I mean, not for the next week, of course.

That's all this possessiveness is about.

"By the way," she says as the car arrives at the store, "how does this end?"

"Us?"

She nods. "The fake engagement."

"I guess we have a fake breakup," I say, even though I hadn't thought out the end of this. Maybe because I hadn't scripted the beginning either. It's all been me flying by the seat of my pants.

"At the end of the week?" she asks, as we reach the gleaming glass doors of the New York institution that's been part of my life for as long as I can remember.

"Yeah, a real fake breakup," I emphasize, before I buy her the ring to seal the deal. A ring that has an expiration date, just like this fake affair that we've now planned the ending for.

The real ending.

* * *

Things I learn about Charlotte in the next hour at Katharine's:

She likes holding hands.

She likes snaking an arm around my waist.

She likes running her fingers through my hair.

She's quite handsy when we're playing pretend—it's downright impressive, her commitment to method acting.

She also has impeccable taste and selects a princess cut two-carat diamond set in a platinum band. "This is the ring I've always wanted," she declares to Nina, my dad's right-hand woman, and I swear Charlotte's going to float away on a cloud of happiness. The woman absolutely sounds like a blushing bride-to-be.

Nina smiles brightly. She's tall and neatly dressed in a silk blouse and gray skirt, and her brown hair is swept into a bun. "Then let's make sure the glass slipper fits you perfectly," she says, and disappears to the back of the store to have the ring sized.

"You're a pro," I say once Nina's out of earshot. Charlotte waves a hand dismissively, and I tell her, "No, seriously. You're going to be accepting an Oscar soon for nailing the role of ecstatic fiancée."

She drags her fingers along a glass case and shrugs, like her performance is no big deal. "I like diamonds. That makes it easy for me."

"Ah, so this is Honest Charlotte in action? And Honest Charlotte loves jewelry?"

She nods. "Honest Charlotte adores princess-cuts and platinum. When my friend Kristen got engaged last year I was thrilled for her, and couldn't stop staring at her princess cut diamond. It was gorgeous, but more importantly, she's so happy, and she's madly in love. Being elated over an engagement ring isn't an emotion I have to fake," she says, meeting my eyes. I can see her sincerity written in them—in this moment, those brown eyes are completely guileless.

She loves the idea of being committed. Maybe not to me. But just in general.

The truth of that emotion is almost too big for me. I gotta go for a joke. "What if it were a pinkie ring, though? What if I wanted to get you a gold pinkie ring with a big, fat rock? Would that fit your style?"

She leans in closer and wiggles her eyebrows. "Thanks for the hint, snookums. Now I know just what to get you for a wedding gift."

Nina returns to tell us the ring should be ready in fifteen minutes. "Thank you. I can't wait," Charlotte says, and now I know she means it. She's telling some sort of truth to Nina.

But I'm lying, and that makes me feel like a bit of a schmuck. I've known Nina for years, and she even babysat for Harper and me when we were younger. She was my dad's first employee when Katharine's started as a small boutique off Park Avenue. A sales clerk, she worked her way up over the years, rising to VP as that one shop grew into an international business. My father has often said that Nina and my mother have helped him make most of his important business decisions in the last thirty years. They're his *key advisors*.

"I'm so thrilled for the two of you, and I'm so glad you're the woman who brought him to one knee," Nina says to Charlotte, who looks away. Nina rests a hip against a display case of diamond tennis bracelets and turns to me, gently swatting my arm. "I still can't believe you're getting married."

"I have to pinch myself too, just to remind me that it's all real," I say, and pinch my forearm, doing my best to ignore the nagging seeds of guilt. I can't let the lying eat away at me. It's all for a good cause, and no one is getting hurt. Besides, I'm not the first dude in the history of the world who needed a fiancée, stat.

"I can remember when you were a wild five-year-old boy like it was yesterday," Nina says, nostalgia glimmering in her eyes.

"I can't believe my dad actually let me visit the store as that crazy five-year-old boy," I say, flashing back to all the hours I've logged in this upscale joint. I know the place inside and out. Five floors of sophistication, glitter, and glamour. Diamonds sparkle behind gleaming glass showcases and atop marble pedestals, and the burgundy carpet is so lush you want to curl up and sleep on it.

Or run circles on it, which is what I did as a kid.

"You were so wound up," Nina says, shaking her finger at me. She smiles, and her gray eyes crinkle when she does.

"How wild was he exactly?" Charlotte asks. I detect a note of mischievous curiosity in her tone. She casts a quick glance at me, and I know what she's doing—fishing for fodder to tease me with at some unsuspecting moment.

Nina laughs delightedly as she answers. "Little Spencer was a handful. Once, when his mother was visiting relatives out of town, Spencer's father brought him into the store an hour before opening, and this little devil child immediately started zipping and zinging around all the cases," she says, weaving a path in the air with her hands to demonstrate.

I cringe, as Charlotte laughs. "I can picture that perfectly."

"Oh, that was only the start of the havoc he tried to wreak. He knocked over a case of rubies once during one of his marathon laps around the store. Another time, he snagged the velvet lining from a display case, and turned it into a cape," she says, and Charlotte's lips twitch in amusement. "But," Nina says, narrowing her eyes and holding up a finger, "I had a solution."

"Benadryl?" Charlotte asks playfully, then squeezes my hand.

I groan inside, knowing what's coming.

"Oh, I wish I could have gotten him to nap while his father was busy in a meeting. Instead, I went to the fancy pet accessories shop down the block, bought a leash, and attached it to the loops of his corduroy pants."

Charlotte's hand flies to her mouth, and I drop my forehead to my palm. There it is. The story I will never live down now. I don't know what's worse—the leash or the corduroy.

"You walked him around the store on a leash?" Charlotte asks, taking her time with each word, wonder in her voice.

Nina nods, proud of her solution. She pats the side of her leg as if she's giving a dog a command, then emits a low whistle. "*C'mere boy,*" she says, laughs shuddering through her. "He loved it. He took to it like a little Cocker Spaniel."

"Amazing. Almost like he's got a little bit of dog in him just waiting to come out," Charlotte says, shaking her head in amusement.

I roll my eyes as the women continue their banter.

"But don't they all? Men, that is," Nina says.

Charlotte nods. "Good thing I like dogs."

"Besides, it was either leash him up, or risk this little hellion breaking all the diamond cases. He's mellowed over the years though. In a good way," Nina says, patting me on the cheek. "And he's mellowing in an even better way now, isn't he?" she says, directing the last words to Charlotte, who gulps and seems to tense. Her eyes widen, and I freeze.

Shit.

This is it.

This is when Charlotte chokes.

"Wouldn't you say so?" Nina continues, prompting Charlotte, who's stock still.

Red starts to streak across her cheeks, and she's about to word-vomit the truth. To blurt it all out in one big, fat confession tied up with a white bow of ridiculous. She might have aced the jewelry selection, but that was easy for her sparkly, jewel-loving heart. This is the hard part, and it shows. Oh crap, does it show in the terror in her eyes.

Her lips start to move, but no sound comes. I squeeze her hand, a reminder that it's her turn to speak. But if she can't form words, I'm going to need to step in. Somehow, she manages a nervous smile, then she winks at Nina, and at last speech returns. "Actually, he's still a hellion. So if you held onto that leash, I might be able to put it to good use."

Nina tosses her head back and cackles. She drops a hand on Charlotte's arm and whispers, "Oh, I do so love the naughty energy of the newly engaged."

She excuses herself to go check on the ring, and Charlotte shoots me a look. "Thought I was going to blow our cover, didn't you?"

I hold up my thumb and forefinger. "You were this close to giving it up, weren't you?"

She arches an eyebrow. "Maybe I wanted you to squirm."

"You evil woman," I say with narrowed eyes.

She dances her fingers up my arm. "Or perhaps I was just processing the fantastic image of you being on a leash," she says, looking like the cat who didn't just eat the canary, but feasted on the bird's whole damn family. "You do know that was basically the best ammunition ever that she just dropped in my hand. The Spencer on a Leash tale. But it got even better when she called you a Cocker Spaniel," she says, the corner of her lips quirking up in a "gotcha" grin.

"What can I say? I guess I was a dog even then." At least I can breathe easily again.

"Do you still like it? Being walked on a leash?" she says, egging me on.

"Is this your way of asking me to participate in kinky, dirty things?"

"No. It's my way of asking how far this fantastic story extends so that if I want to mention it while we're at the bar, or out with Nick or Kristen, or your sister, that I get it right," she says, miming walking a dog.

But that's not how I see things going. Not at all. Just so she knows how I like these scenarios to play out, I lean in closer, brush her hair away from her shoulder, and whisper, "If anyone's getting tied up, it's you. And it won't be with a leash. It'll be with a scarf, or stockings, or that black hot-as-fuck thong you put on because I made you so wet you had to change. I'd wrap it around your wrists, nice and tight, then pin them behind your back until you beg me to touch you."

Her breath catches.

She trembles, and a shiver runs through her body. She grips the front of my shirt, her fingertips curling around a button. And holy fuck... she likes the idea of being tied up. I can feel it in the air. In the way protons and electrons are buzzing. In the sexual energy that's radiating off her body.

I inhale.

It smells like chemistry.

And I have no clue what to make of it.

I don't even know why I just said that, since I'm not supposed to be thinking about screwing her, let alone tying her up.

Good thing Nina returns moments later with the ring. "A rush sizing job for my most special customers," she says with a smile. Charlotte holds out her hand, and I slide the diamond onto her ring finger, meeting her eyes for a second. I try to read them, to see if she thinks this is as sur-real as I do—me, the New York City playboy, putting a ring on it.

Even a temporary one.

Maybe this is weird for her too.

As I study her face, I can't tell at first from her serious expression how she's feeling to wear an engagement ring for the first time. Then I see it in her big, brown eyes, as a flicker of sadness passes over them. My heart lurches, and I figure she's remembering that ten months ago she was about to be engaged to a man who wound up breaking her heart.

Good thing I won't be the one making her look that way ever. I don't have the power to hurt her like that.

I drop a quick kiss on her cheek, then hand over my platinum card and spend close to ten thousand dollars on a ring. When we go to work that night, she doesn't wear it.

CHAPTER TEN

The next afternoon, I'm watching as a little white ball soars high in the air, then lands with a plunk on fake grass about fifteen feet away.

"Dude, you suck," I tell Nick.

"Well aware of that."

He grabs another ball, sets it down on the tee, and swings his club. When he makes contact, the ball sails so damn high, it nearly hits the top of the black net, then smacks the long path of green that extends below like a dock over the Hudson River. Two white cruise ships are moored next to the driving range, and nothing but blue skies stretch above us. We're at Chelsea Piers, where he's working on his golf game.

"Hate to break it to you, but I doubt your new boss is going to be terribly impressed with your swing. Maybe you can convince him to play softball with us instead."

He scoffs. "Not likely. The man is obsessed with golf, and word is he plays favorites and gives better time slots to the showrunners who keep up with him on the course."

"That's insane. But if that's true, you need less shoulder. More hips," I tell him, since I dabbled in golf in high school. I don't talk about it much. Makes me sound too snooty. Or too old. But if it helps my buddy, I'll call up the old golf skill book for him.

Nick raises his face and stares at me through his black hipster glasses, his brown hair flopping down on his forehead. "Don't you dare put your hands on my hips to show me."

I crack up, holding up my hands in surrender. "You can count on that never happening," I say, as I move out of the way of his next attempt.

He does better this time, and the ball arcs neatly over the grass.

"There you go," I say. "Write that into your next episode. Mr. Orgasm's buddy saves his ass from embarrassing himself with his golf swing in front of the new boss."

Nick Hammer is a rock star in the TV world. Back in high school, he was the quiet geek bent over his notebook sketching dirty comic strips that he posted online. Ten years later, he turned his talent and his concept into an animated TV show—*The Adventures of Mr. Orgasm*, a hilarious and filthy show that airs late at night on the cable network Comedy Nation. The hero is an animated caped crusader who bestows orgasmic pleasure on womankind. Pretty sure it was wish fulfillment for Nick back in high school. Now, art imitates life and vice versa. He's still got a quiet side, but women notice him. He's hit the weights since our teenage days, inked up his arms with tattoos he designed himself, and found the guts to finally start talking to the opposite sex. The result? Pure magic. The man's a total tomcat, and I suspect the glasses and unassuming I-once-was-a-geek-now-I'm-a-star persona helps his cause with the ladies.

"And how exactly does the *coming* come into play in this storyline you propose?" he asks dryly.

I shrug and clap him on the shoulder. "Don't know. That's why you, my man, are the writer. It's your job to figure out how the Os fit into the show. Speaking of storylines, I need a little help with something," I say, getting to the heart of this quick detour I've made to see him this afternoon.

He sets down his club, and crooks his finger. "It's called the G-spot. You find it inside a woman. When you hit it at just the right angle, she comes harder than she ever has before. Need anything else?"

I pretend to bang a drumstick as soundtrack to his punchline, then I tell him about my new temporary relationship status.

After he laughs, guffaws, and chuckles over my predicament, he asks, "Is this your way of asking me to be your best man? Will the wedding be fake, too?"

I laugh and shake my head. "There won't be a wedding. Ever. But this is what I need. When we have our softball game next weekend, my dad will be there, and his buyer will be there. All I need is for you to act like you knew I was into her. If it comes up, don't act surprised or suspicious." My dad runs a mixed-age softball team sponsored by Katharine's, and he recruited both Nick and me for his team this year. Nick's softball swing is worlds better than his golf swing.

He nods several times, like he's taking in my directive, then he strokes his chin. "Let me get this straight. What you're saying is, I should behave like I'm perfectly capable of backing up the latest bullshit of yours. Okay. I think I can do that."

I roll my eyes. "That's why I depend on you. The bottomless well of sarcasm."

"It matches yours," he says with a smirk.

"I need to take off, since I have this dinner thing tonight. I'll catch you later."

I start to head out, when he calls out to me. "Does this mean I can't put the moves on Charlotte now?"

My shoulders tense for a moment and that fiery burst of possessiveness returns with a vengeance, like a red-tailed hawk swooping down from the sky, big-ass claws brandished. I remind myself he's joking. That's what he does. And I'm not the least bit jealous or possessive. The hawk turns into a dove. "Just for the next week or so," I say. "Then she's all yours."

But those words feel all wrong coming out of my month. Even if she's not mine, she can't be *his*. And I'm not a motherfucking bird of peace.

"I always thought you two would make a cute couple," he says in a sugar-sweet voice.

As I walk off, he makes mock kissing sounds. I'm pretty sure he's singing the kissing tree song, and it's definitely my cue to put him in the rearview mirror.

Besides, I need to get in character for tonight.

Because this is all an act.

Nothing more.

CHAPTER ELEVEN

The steak is delicious, the Caesar salad tasty, and the red wine smooth.

Like the conversation.

So far, so good. It's been jewelry, private schools, softball leagues, and how great the weather is. Can you spell getting-away-with-it?

Oh, and after we arrived at the restaurant, the Offermans all bestowed their requisite 'congratulations' on my bride-to-be and me, as she flashed her ring, and the women oohed and aahed. My sister, too. Her congrats was the biggest of all; so was her hug, as she pulled me into her loving, sisterly vice and breathed, barely audible, in my ear, "You can't fool me. But I've got your back."

Guess you can't trick a magician. She's been trained to detect sleight of hand, and she spotted mine in seconds.

"Thanks. I owe you."

"You do. Especially since I still haven't forgiven you for the Santa Claus incident when I was ten," she hissed, before breaking apart and flashing a smile for the camera.

But the reporter from *Metropolis Life and Times* didn't seem to catch on, nor did he last for long here at the private room in McCoy's. I suspect he was an intern, which confirms this will be some sort of puff piece. A young guy, he lobbed a few questions at my dad and Mr. Offerman, about the handover of the family-owned business, then snapped some pictures of the clan and took off. Probably so he doesn't miss his bedtime.

Easy as pie.

Now we're finishing our meal at this midtown steak restaurant that exudes class and ambiance with its crisp white tablecloths, oak tables, soft lighting, and waiters in suits. I slide my knife through the filet mignon and do a double take at something in the corner of my vision. Mr. Offerman's oldest daughter, Emily, is seated across from me. She twirls a strand of her long black hair and looks at me.

Uh-oh.

I recognize that stare. It's the kind women give from across the bar when they're flirting with you. Worry shimmies through me. Is she batting her eyelashes, now?

Averting my gaze, I take a bite of the steak, chew it, and swallow roughly. I grab my wineglass and down more of the red liquid. Something slides across the toe of my shoe.

Something that feels distinctly like Foot of a Young Lady.

No.

No fucking way.

Is Emily playing footsie with me?

My chest tightens.

I yank my foot away.

My sister laughs out loud.

The stinking little prankster. She's sitting next to Emily.

My mother turns to Harper and smiles brightly. "Something funny?"

She nods, her red ponytail bouncing as she reins in a grin. "Just remembering this funny joke I heard."

"Care to share? Or is it inappropriate?" my mother asks, voice laced with politeness. She wants this dinner to go well for my dad, too. She's no stick in the mud. If Harper has a good, clean joke, my mom will want to hear it. The woman loves laughing.

My sister sets down her fork. "It's completely appropriate. In fact, it's perfect for Spencer now," Harper says, her eyes lasered in on me. She clears her throat. She's got the attention of the whole table. I sit ramrod straight, nerves skittering through me because I have no clue what she's up to. She said she'd keep my secret, but she's also been looking for a way to stick it to me ever since I told her Santa Claus wasn't real, and that as a fifth grader she was too old to still believe in him. With wet eyes and a tear-stained face, she swore she'd get back at me for ruining her greatest dream.

She better not be exacting her revenge now. If she is, I will dangle her upside down over the banister until she cries uncle. Oh, wait. That was ten-year-old Spencer thinking. The mature me would *never* do that. Instead, I'll just break out the old family photo album the next time she brings a date home. Show off her second grade haircut. That she gave herself.

"Can't wait to hear it," I say, leaning back in my chair.

Bring it on, sis.

She raises her chin and launches into her joke. "Why can't Ray Charles see his friends?"

"Why?" Mrs. Offerman asks curiously, knitting her brow. She mouths to herself, "because he's blind," and seems pleased she got the answer in advance.

My sister pauses, tilts her head, and stares straight at me. "Because he's married."

Harper has the whole table laughing. Well, the over-twenty crowd. Mr. Offerman's daughters hardly chuckle, but Harper doesn't need to amuse them. She had them eating out of her hand earlier in the night when she was discussing pop music and tips for taking better selfies, including points for—get this—video selfies.

"Do you think that'll happen to you soon, Spencer?" my sister asks, batting her eyelashes at me as she props her chin in her hands.

She is such a devil.

"Nah, Charlotte is cool," I say as I slide my shoe closer to Harper under the table, and try to kick her. I mean, tap her foot lightly. But instead, Emily yelps.

"Ouch, that hurt," she whines.

Oh fuck. Wrong girl.

"What happened, dear?" Mrs. Offerman snaps her gaze to her oldest daughter. She's a petite woman, and has spent most of the meal fussing over her family members.

"Someone just kicked me under the table," Emily says, annoyed.

Her mother turns those watchful blue eyes to my side of the table, scanning for the kicking culprit. I wince inside. I can't believe I've fucked this up already, and it's all because of my sister.

I race through possible excuses, but before I latch onto one, Charlotte pipes in, placing her hand on her heart in apology. "I'm so sorry, Emily. That was me. When Spencer drives me crazy, I kick him under the table. And, being a man, he does that often, even though I still adore him. This time though, I slipped and kicked you. I'm sorry," she says with the sweetest smile, and I could kiss her. I could fucking kiss her.

So I do. I clasp my hand on her cheek. "I deserved it. I love that you keep me in check, honey bear," I say, then press a soft kiss to her lips.

She kisses me back for a few seconds, a chaste, sweet kiss, but even so, it's nearly enough for me to forget the whole table full of people. All I want is more of this fake kissing. More tongue, more lips, more teeth.

More contact.

More *her*.

Exactly what I can't be wanting.

Clapping begins. I end the kiss to see my sister leading the cheers. "You two are the cutest couple. When is the wedding?"

Oh.

That detail.

My mother's eyes shine with excitement. "Oh yes, will it be a summer wedding?"

"We're thinking spring," Charlotte says, once again seamlessly taking the reins. "Perhaps May. Maybe at an art gallery. Or a museum. The Museum of Modern Art has such lovely sculpture gardens for weddings."

"Oh, that would be a gorgeous location," Mrs. Offerman says, the kicking incident now in a galaxy far, far away. She cups her hand over the side of her mouth so her girls can't see her. "I've already been scoping out locations for their nuptials, even though those are years away. But you can never start too early."

Mr. Offerman clasps his hand on top of hers. "It's a good hobby for you, dear. It gets you out of the kitchen."

I straighten my spine. Are we in the fifties here? "Out of the kitchen?"

My father clears his throat, his voice booming over mine. "Kate, what do you think of the sculpture garden?" he says to my mother, and that's my cue to zip my lips. "You've always loved the Museum of Modern Art."

"It's a stunning location, and I think Charlotte and Spencer's wedding will be beautiful wherever they choose to hold it. Charlotte, I know you're close to your own mother, but I'm here for any planning help you need. I adore weddings."

Mrs. Offerman weighs in again, locking her gaze with Charlotte. "Your mother must be so thrilled. Will she be planning it for you?"

Charlotte's expression turns perplexed, and she furrows her brow. "I'm sure she'll help."

"Of course she'll help, dear. She'll do more than help. Is she nearby?"

"My parents live in Connecticut."

"What else would she be doing but helping plan the special day?" Mrs. Offerman says with a look of utter surprise, as if she can't comprehend any scenario but the one where Charlotte's mom spends every waking hour barking commands at florists and issuing orders at swank reception halls.

"She's pretty busy with work," Charlotte says.

"Oh. Work?" That seems to confuse the woman. "What does she do?"

"She's a surgeon at a hospital in New Haven."

Mrs. Offerman's eyebrows shoot into her hairline, her eyes widening to beach-ball size. "How interesting. And your father?"

"He's a nurse," Charlotte says, and her tone is so completely dry that I start to crack up, but manage to suck in the sound and clamp my lips together once more.

"Really? I thought he was a doctor, too?" my mother says, genuinely surprised, as she should be, since Charlotte is fucking lying right now. It is killing me, absolutely killing me to hold all this laugher inside my throat.

Charlotte smacks her forehead. "My bad. He started as nurse, but he worked his way up, at my mother's encouragement, and became a doctor, too." This time she is telling the whole truth, and the look on Mrs. Offerman's face is priceless. It's as if she's never heard of a male nurse, and certainly not one who became a doctor at his wife's urging. Mr. Offerman appears even more flummoxed.

The silence spreads. The table goes quiet for a moment. The clink of glasses and the jangling slide of forks against china is the only sound in the private room.

"To the happy couple," my father says, rescuing the table from any more chatter about the roles of men and women by raising his glass.

"Hear, hear. Who doesn't love a wedding? It's our favorite thing, isn't it?" Mr. Offerman says to Dad with a wink that says, *now we're two men celebrating what feeds our business.*

His daughters raise their soda glasses, and I hold up my wine glass, clinking first with Charlotte. A faint noise comes from under the table, like a light *thunk*. She flashes me a grin, and there's something very private in her expression, something that says we have a secret. Then, I know what it is. Because this time, there's no doubt who's touching who. It's her toes sliding over the top of my shoes. Then along my lower leg. Now higher, and it's crazy, truly crazy, that Charlotte's toes along my leg feel so damn good.

The kind of good where I want to grab her hand, tug her into the bathroom, push her up against the wall, and hike up that skirt. The kind where I discover what kind of panties she's wearing tonight, and if they're already damp with her arousal.

But that. Can't. Happen.

Must be all the wine.

"We should go to MoMA tomorrow," Mrs. Offerman says to my mom. "Emily plans to study art history in college next year." Emily raises an eyebrow, like she disagrees with that notion. "And you can check out the gardens, Kate."

"What a lovely idea," my mother, ever the diplomat, says.

Mrs. Offerman locks eyes with Charlotte. "Would you like to join us?"

"Absolutely." Charlotte squeezes my hand. "We'll both be there."

"Can't wait," I say, because any other answer could be cause for dismemberment.

I finish my glass of wine, and as the conversation heads in another direction, so does Charlotte's foot, as she slides it back into her shoe. I'm grateful, because if I get aroused by a foot, I might need to get myself checked out to make sure I haven't reverted to preteen turn-on levels.

After dessert and coffee, I pull my sister away from the table, far enough from the others to have a word with her.

"Harper, seriously. You've got to be on my side. You were so close to serving it up."

"Oh, please. I was not. I was only having fun. You know I've got your back, and always do," she says, like I'd be crazy to think otherwise. But crazy feels like my new normal this weekend.

"I know. Just be in on this with me. Not against me," I say, a dash of desperation in my voice. Who am I kidding? It's not a dash. It's a full fucking serving.

She laughs. "You're so pathetic when you need something. Where's the Spencer who dangled me over the banister when I was eight?"

I adopt a look of shock. "I thought you were six when that happened?"

"Even worse." She pulls me in for a hug. "It's okay. I won't rat you out. But I hope you know what you're doing."

"Don't worry. I got this."

"You better. And you better be careful." She turns her voice to a threatening whisper, and grasps my shirt. "But some day, when you least expect it, I will take my revenge for Santa." Her grip tightens and her voice goes even quieter. "Watch your ten o'clock—Emily is making eyes at you. She has it bad for you already."

Emily rises from the table, staring at the phone in her hand.

"Wrong," I say, as I break the embrace. "She's just zoned out on her screen, texting friends probably."

But it turns out my sister isn't wrong, because Emily is definitely looking at me now. Her eyes hook into mine, and her tongue darts out, licking her lips.

Harper laughs, then brandishes imaginary claws. "Meow. I smell a catfight."

I shake my head. Charlotte is hardly the type for a catfight.

My fake fiancée walks past Emily, and the younger girl roams her eyes over Charlotte like she's studying her, waiting to pounce. Her hand shoots out, and she grabs Charlotte's arm. Shit, Harper was right. Fisticuffs are about to start. I'm momentarily torn between the sheer rubbernecking fascination of watching the scene unfold, and the impulse to stop a tussle.

"Oh my God, I love your shoes," Emily says, a huge adoring smile on her face. "Where did you get them?"

Whew. Emily was only checking out Charlotte's footwear. The two of them gab about fashion and clothes and designers, and Charlotte handles it all with aplomb.

I don't know why she doubted herself earlier today.

She fucking rocks. She can be my fake fiancée anytime.

CHAPTER TWELVE

Charlotte lets out a big breath. She wipes her hand across her forehead. "After that performance, and this long day, I need a drink," she says when we slide into a cab. "Or two."

"You and me both." I tap her knee with my knuckles, then tell the driver to head downtown. "By the way, *nurse*. Fucking brilliant."

We knock fists. "And it wasn't even a lie. It was just a, how shall we say, delayed admission of the truth."

"Honestly, I'm giving you an A for perfect timing with your delivery tonight."

"Why thank you," she says, playfully. "I look forward to my report card."

I pretend to hand one to her.

She mimes opening it, then reads. "I see I earned straight As."

I shake my head. "A-plus. The nurse comment counts as extra credit. See?" I stab a finger at the invisible report card, as if I'm pointing it out.

She laughs and grabs my arm. "I couldn't help myself. Her comments were so old-fashioned."

My mom stayed home with Harper and me as kids, so I'm totally on board with a mom working out of the house or taking care of the kids. Whatever works for her. In Mom's case, she raised us, and she also advised my father on his business. Through it all, he treated her like a queen in some ways and an equal in all ways. That's how it should be, whatever choice a woman makes.

"Speaking of old-fashioned, want to try Gin Joint?" I ask, naming a new bar in Chelsea that's getting rave reviews, especially for its old-fashioned made with gin.

"Yes. I've been up since six a.m.," she says, then pouts her lips like a movie star of olden days and speaks in a husky, sexy tone. "But I'm still in the mood for a nightcap."

Soon we walk through a red door into a garden-level bar with soft, sultry music piped in overhead, and wine red, royal blue, and deep purple velvet couches. The place has a New Orleans–style ambiance—rich, dark, and moody.

Charlotte sinks down onto a couch, dropping her purse by her side, relaxation evident in her pose. I order for us, returning with her old-fashioned and a bourbon on the rocks for me.

"To Honest Charlotte," I say, lifting my glass.

"To Cocker Spaniel Spencer," she says, then takes a drink. She moans after the first sip and taps her glass. "That is divine. Try it."

She hands me the glass, and I take a drink. My taste buds do a jig. "Wow. Can we steal their recipe?"

She laughs. "Just like the time we went to Speakeasy," she says, her eyes twinkling with the memory of how we went into business together. We were celebrating the sale of Boyfriend Material at the opening of a new bar in midtown. We'd ordered the bar's signature cocktail, the Purple Snow Globe, which went on to become a big hit as a packaged drink sold in grocery stores. It was so damn good, we'd both pointed to our drinks at the same time, and said "Let's steal this recipe."

"Jinx, you owe me a drink," we'd then said in unison.

That had sealed the deal on our plans. In college, we were beer snobs, and we used to joke at parties that we'd open our own bar someday, and we'd kick ass at it because we could tell the difference between quality beer and the swill from a keg. Hardly a special skill, but even so, that was what got us rolling.

Once we graduated, we went in different directions work wise, even though we stayed close friends. I launched my app, and Charlotte snagged a plum gig in business development at a Fortune 500 company. The hours were ruthless, though, the environment was cutthroat, and there wasn't a single ounce of enjoyment. She was miserable but determined not to wallow in it, so she started making plans to do what she loved—run a business based on fun, being social, and hanging out with friends. When she gave notice, she asked me if I was ready to do what we'd talked about the night we'd vowed never to drink keg beer.

"I've been squirreling away my yearly bonuses. Want to open a bar in midtown with me?"

Flush with cash from the sale, and ready for a new adventure, I'd said yes in seconds. "Can we name the bar after the dogs we had as kids?"

"Hell yeah."

The rest is history. The Lucky Spot is profitable and has expanded to three locations, and we have a blast running it together.

Charlotte and I reminisce about our early days in business as Gin Joint fills up. The door opens, and a group of pretty, sexy ladies wearing slinky jeans and heels that go on forever pour in. Somewhere in the back of my mind, a part of me says to check them out, but the thought vanishes almost as quickly as it appears.

Charlotte finishes her old-fashioned just as my bourbon disappears. We move on to seconds as we talk about our most memorable customers over the years. The conversation is free and easy, and it reminds me of why we work so well as friends, and why it's so much better for our friendship if we don't ever practice kissing again. Because I don't want to give this up. She's the person I can most be myself with, and I like just chilling here with her. We didn't do a ton of this when Bradley Dipstick was in the picture.

Like she can read my mind, Charlotte sighs happily and says, "I missed doing this with you when I was with that jackass."

"I was thinking the same thing."

She tilts her head and looks up at me. "Really?" The expression on her face is one of wonder and surprise. "So it works, then?"

"What works?" I ask curiously.

She runs a finger along the side of my hair. "The device I implanted in your head so I could read your mind," she says in mock seriousness.

I laugh and squeeze her shoulder. "You got me. Next round on me."

"The entire night better be on you."

"It is. And yes, I missed this, too—hanging with you when you were with him."

"Going to your house. Binge watching TV shows, eating gummy bears or lemonheads, and drinking tequila or wine, depending on what we decided went best together."

"We really are quite savvy at our candy-liquor pairings."

"We are." Charlotte sighs happily and scoots closer, almost like she's going to cuddle with me. "You know, this might sound weird, but I'm glad I caught him screwing that woman. Buying a place with him would have been such a mistake. It was like someone was looking out for me, in a weird way. Does that sound crazy?"

"Not at all."

"If I were with him—engaged to him and living with him—I wouldn't be able to do this with you."

At first I'm sure she means hanging out. But when I feel a brush of her hand against my leg, I wonder if she means something else.

I look down, and her palm is spread across my thigh. *Interesting.* I'm honestly not sure when that happened, or why I didn't notice it before, but her hand is warm, and it feels good, and I suppose I'm getting used to her touching me. Maybe that's why I didn't realize she's been touching me the last few minutes as we've been chatting. I've quickly grown accustomed to her hands on my body.

When the waitress strolls by, Charlotte calls her over, and orders a gin and tonic. By the time it arrives five minutes later, Charlotte's hand is no longer resting on my thigh. It's moving. She strokes little lines along my leg, and this isn't just handsy anymore. This is something else entirely.

I'm caught off guard and completely unprepared for this side of Charlotte—the nighttime, after hours Charlotte, who is very much touching me like we are together, even though there's no audience now.

"Spencer," she says, and her voice is all floaty and happy, "I'm so glad we went into business together."

Okay, that makes sense. She's in one of those happy-go-lucky tipsy moods where she gushes about life being good. I can handle this. She takes a sip of her drink, sets down the glass, and shifts closer. As she moves nearer, so do her fingertips, as they migrate higher up my leg.

Whoa.

Was not expecting all this hand action, nor the subtle path she's taking.

"Yeah. Me, too."

Her fingers brush higher on the fabric of my pants. She's getting friendlier. Much friendlier. *Just how strong are these drinks?*

"I was so miserable before we started it, and now I love what I do," she says, and her hand on my thigh suddenly acquires a mind of its own. Or hormones of its own. Because it is on a one-way path to my dick. And it's like someone cranked up the heat in the bar. "Do you know why else I'm glad I'm not with Bradley?"

"Why?" I ask carefully, as those nimble, eager fingers inch closer. I'm *en fuego*. My neck is hot. My hair might be up in flames. I could melt polar caps right about now.

"Because I'm having a great time playing pretend with you," she says, and her right breast presses against my arm. She's so soft, and I'm dying to know what her breasts feel like in my hands, how she'd respond to my fingers tracing circles across the sensitive flesh, the noises she'd make when I suck a nipple into my mouth.

How hard her nipples get from my lips.

There I go again.

Exactly where I shouldn't be.

Her fingers are not inches, not centimeters, but now millimeters from the outline of my dick.

I know what to do, and at the same time, I don't have a clue. My instincts tell me the moves to make, how to touch, how to kiss, how to fuck. But it's like a page from the playbook is missing. A whole damn chapter even. Because this is Charlotte, and our situation is beyond bizarre. We're friends and business partners. We're fake lovers who aren't fucking. Yesterday, we were sober and practicing kissing, and tonight we were performing for an audience.

Now all bets are off. It's just us, and yet we're still touching.

Neither one of us is operating at top-notch brainpower, though. I'm tipsy, but she's highly buzzed. That's got to be where all this persistent contact is coming from. It's like the bar is trying to seduce us, to weave its spell on us. It's dark, and everyone around us is touching, arms around waists, hands in pockets, lips on neck. Gin Joint is pulsing with dirty thoughts. It's beating with the promise of midnight, and sex after dark.

My breath flees my chest when her fingers touch my hard-on. Her eyes light up, like she's opening a gift, and that's exactly how I want a woman to feel, but precisely how Charlotte should not fucking feel.

"Charlotte," I say, my voice a harsh warning.

"Spencer," she whispers, her lips pouty and sexy as she lingers on the last letter. When she does that, all I can see is her lips on my cock, her blonde hair spilling across my legs, her head bobbing up and down. It's a glorious image, and a goddamn dangerous one.

The tempo shifts again when she simply rests her head on my shoulder, and returns her hands to her lap.

Like she turned off the light switch.

"I just like hanging out with you," she says, her eyes fluttering, like she's sleepy.

"I like it, too," I rasp out. "And you're tired."

"I know. Long day. My pillow is calling out to me."

Great. Fucking great. I'm turned on, and she's sliding into the snooze zone. Her hands have settled down, her touchy-feely side has subsided, and I'm left with a massive fucking erection, and my best friend's sexy-as-sin body snuggled by my side on a velvet couch.

Fifteen minutes later, we get in a cab. I give the driver Charlotte's address, because I want to make sure my happy, tipsy, tired friend gets home safely. After the word "Lexington" leaves my mouth, I turn to look at her, and everything happens in a wild blur.

CHAPTER THIRTEEN

Her arms are around my neck and her mouth claims mine. She kisses me furiously, like a storm, a lightning storm of kisses raining down from the sky, bursting with heat and sparks and thunder.

She's buzzed. I can feel it in the loose, languid way she moves, in the softness of her limbs, and in the panting in her breath. I taste gin on her lips, and the liquor has never tasted better in my life than when it's mixed with Charlotte. Everything about her bombards my senses—her taste, her scent, her breath. I smell honey on her skin—she used honey blossom from that collection she showed me. Knowing this small detail about her, where this intoxicating scent comes from, makes the blood roar in my veins. Makes me want to know what she'll smell like tomorrow. How she'll taste the next day. When she gets out of the shower, what scent she'll rub into her body, and whether it will drive me wild, too.

This honey smell is spectacular. Heady and bewitching and all *her*, and I know whatever she puts on the next day and the next will turn me on with the same raging intensity, because she is so fucking alluring.

Especially when she sucks on my lip like that. I groan and rope my arms around her, yanking her closer. She's climbed up on me, straddling me in the back of the cab as it slings us up the avenue, the lights of late-night Manhattan whipping by.

She says my name again on a smoky moan. It sounds like an orgasm as it leaves her red lips. "*Spencer.* I want you," she whispers in my ear. "You got me so wet from that kiss yesterday. I'm so wet right now, too. Everything you do turns me on."

Oh God. Oh hell. Oh, fucking save me from myself.

There is no way. I need to press the brakes. This car is speeding out of control. It's going to crash in a fiery blaze. I have to stop it.

"Charlotte," I warn, and I try to peel her off me, but what's this now? She's lifted up her skirt and positioned herself on the outline of my cock, and this is sweet, unholy torture of the highest degree. I breathe out hard as I gaze down at her. The cab slows at a light, and neither one of us gives a shit that the cab driver is three feet away. I can't care about anything but the pure heat sizzling over my skin as she grinds against me. Her wet panties rub against my erection, and her lips are everywhere on me, like a sensual assault that comes so close to breaking me down. Her mouth moves to my neck, my chin, my jaw, as she travels to my ear. She slides her teeth across my earlobe and nips.

I moan and grip her hips harder. I fucking love it. I love everything she does. She flicks her tongue against the shell of my ear, and I might as well just wave the white flag and admit defeat, because she's found my weak spot, and she seems to know it. She kisses me there, and every sweep of her tongue makes me harder, makes me want to haul her up to her home, throw her on her bed, slide into her and show her that if she can drive me crazy with a kiss, I can make her scream in pleasure with my cock.

She raises her hips, slams back down onto me, and whispers, "When I felt you on my couch it drove me wild. Completely wild."

Her hand snakes between us, and she grabs my cock.

I'm electrified. Every inch of me buzzes with thousands of watts of power because she touches me through my pants. Her eyes shine with pure, unbridled lust as if she's realizing how much there is of me, and, I hope, how much she wants me. Fuck, I want her to have it all.

Right now.

"I want to know how you feel inside me," she murmurs.

A thousand responses fill my head. *It'll feel better than anything you've ever had. Unzip my pants, wrap your hands around my cock, and let me take you for the ride of your life. You'll see stars, mountains will move, and the earth will shake.*

The simplest answer, though, is the one I'm dying to utter.

God, I want to fuck you so fucking badly right now.

But thankfully, those aren't the words that escape my lips. Somehow, the rational portion of my brain knows better. The gentleman inside me fights his way out, manages to squirm his way up, and resume control from the manwhore.

Charlotte is buzzed, and I will not take advantage of Buzzed Honest Charlotte.

"You're drunk, Snuffaluffagus. Let's get you in your jammies and put you to bed," I say as I grip her hips to lift her off me.

She's faster. She moves quickly, parking herself in her seat with more agility that I expected. She sneers, "I'm not drunk," and it comes out surprisingly crisp and clear.

I'm not going to argue this point right now. Drunk or not, that was a far too risky moment. The cab slows at the next light, and she yawns loudly, covering her mouth. Her head sinks on my shoulder. Soon, I'm unlocking her door, carrying her to her bed, and sliding off her shoes. She murmurs something as her eyes flutter closed.

"Water," I say. "You need water."

"Mmm. That sounds delish," she says sleepily.

I head to the kitchen, fill a cold glass, and bring it to her. "Sit up," I tell her, and she manages to scoot back in bed. I hand her the glass. She downs most of it. "Drink it all. I'll leave another glass on your nightstand. Drink that one when you wake up in the middle of the night to pee."

Nodding, she sets down the glass. She throws her arms around me, and tugs me into bed. She tries to pull me next to her.

"I have to go."

"Stay with me. Please," she says, patting the soft, comfy bed. "Just sleep next to me. That's all I want."

Sleep next to her? With this boner? With her wild hands crawling all over my body? No way. I'm not that strong. I'm not that good.

"I need to go. I've got to feed my cat." It sounds like the lamest excuse in the world, but it's actually true.

There's a flash of hurt in her eyes. Maybe even disappointment. Then it passes, and she smiles faintly. "Good night, Captain Fiancé. Give the pussy a kiss for me."

Oh, how I would absolutely love to.

Her head hits the pillow, and in seconds she's snoring. It's so fucking cute, the little sounds she makes. I scratch my head—how is it possible that her snores are adorable? But they are. I stand and look at her in the dark, the moonlight streaking across her covers, cutting a crisscross pattern through the blinds. Her blonde hair is spread over her white pillow, her blouse slinks down her shoulder, revealing a cherry red bra, and the skirt of her dress rides up her thighs. I could undress her like they do in the movies, or I could leave her in her clothes.

Undressing her feels like a violation. Instead, I do what I told her I would. I fill her glass of water and leave it on the nightstand. I open her medicine cabinet, grab two aspirin, just in case, and place them next to the glass. I hunt for some paper, and I find a Post-It notepad in her kitchen and a pen in the utensil drawer.

I write: *Two aspirin in the morning, and call me when you get up. I need to take you out for the final hangover prevention step.*

I leave, and I should earn a commendation for self-restraint. I'm going to contact the Guys' Committee and let them know what I accomplished tonight in the resistance category. I'll fully expect a gold medal in the morning and, frankly, an awards ceremony, considering the level of difficulty.

A cab blows past me on Lexington, but I don't shoot my arm into the air to flag it down. Instead, I turn south and walk home, even though I'm many, many blocks away. I need the time and the space and the distance from those five minutes in the cab when I wanted to fuck my best friend's brains out.

This city should take my mind off Charlotte, so I soak it in—the bodegas peddling fruit and flowers, the Chinese restaurants offering greasy noodles, the twenty-four-hour pharmacies selling anything and everything. I cut across town, surrounded by throngs of people, so many still out late at night.

But when I unlock my door at one a.m., I'm still turned on. The walk didn't work. I'm horny as hell. I feel like I've taken Charlotte Viagra, and this hard-on is a cruel and unusual punishment for lusting so badly after my best friend.

Fido meows, then stretches up to greet me, his paws on my leg.

"Hungry?"

His tail twitches. I head to the kitchen, open his bag, and scoop out some cat food. It's this all-natural, organic, eat-like-your-ancestors food. Harper got it for him when I took him in, telling me that store-bought food wouldn't cut it. My man is addicted to it; maybe it makes him feel like a tiger.

I set the bowl down, and he purrs as he eats. The dude is so satisfied from a bowl of dry kibble, and a knot of jealousy tightens in my belly. Great. Now I'm envious of my cat because his life is simpler than mine. *Note to self: Go to the store tomorrow and order up some perspective, because you're losing yours.*

I head to the bathroom. I wash my face, brush my teeth, and try to put the evening behind me. Look, it's not hard to turn down a drunk girl, because that's just wrong. But it was hard, for some unknown fucking reason, to turn down *her.* Those things she was saying. Those wicked, dirty words falling from her red lips. They torched a path up my body. They stirred something inside me. Some wish. Some want.

That kiss on the street was one thing.

The session on her couch was entirely another.

But the cab was a whole new wrinkle. She just combusted, like a rocket of lust, firing off in every direction, jumping me, climbing me, grinding on me.

I wanted it all.

I wanted her.

I still do.

I undress and toss my clothes into the hamper in my closet. Naked, I get into bed, turn off the lights, and park both hands behind my head. Faint sounds of late Saturday night in New York filter through the window, even from six stories high. Shoes clicking on cobblestoned streets, friends laughing, cabs stopping and letting out customers, then picking up other fares.

Even after zoning in on all that, I'm still insanely aroused.

What the fuck am I supposed to do with this erection? Hammer some nails? Bang some wood? This is like a punishment erection. It's got its own blood supply.

I shut my eyes, squeeze them tight, and press my palms into the back of my skull, resisting.

Because I can't go there.

Can't jack off to her. Can't do it. Won't do it. Won't ruin the friendship by going that far. We've already done more than we should, and if we go further, we'll lose everything she was saying was good at the bar tonight. She's my steady, reliable, fantastic friend. She gives me hell, and she makes me laugh, and I can't risk losing her by fucking her.

Or even thinking of fucking her.

But I am dying here. My skin is on fire, and my brain is stuck on repeat—*sex, sex, sex.*

I've got to do something about this persistent hard-on that has been working overtime today, like it signed up for a twenty-four-hour shift. I pad out to the living room, grab my laptop, and return to my bed, flipping open the screen.

Women. Lots of women. Hot lesbian porn. That's what I need. Something totally removed from the last two days of torrential lust. Like, two hot chicks in stockings banging each other. No Tumblr gifs for me, please. I need video, and I know where to find it.

In seconds, a gorgeous redhead in black stockings and garters walks into a dimly lit living room. Perfect. Parking the laptop on the covers, I stretch out my naked body on my bed, my head propped up on a couple of pillows so I can enjoy the front-row seat.

A smoking hot brunette joins her, wearing only white thigh-highs and heels. This will do the trick, thank you very much. I take my dick in my hand and stroke. Moving my palm down my shaft, I skim lightly at first, down to my balls, which are heavy and aching.

Just what the doctor ordered. I'm going to enjoy every single second of this jerk. I tighten my grip. My dick is throbbing in my palm, but I'm thrilled to be on the road to imminent relief as the women move to their couch and get it on.

This is perfect, because neither looks like Charlotte. They kiss, and my skin grows hotter all over as I watch these naked beauties. Their mouths devour each other, and the redhead cups the brunette's full, round tits in her hands. The brunette moans and slides her fingers between the redhead's pussy lips. My shaft grows thicker as I watch the brunette's finger flick across all that wetness.

My breath hitches, and I groan.

Loudly.

Imagining how hot and wet her pussy is.

All nice and slick and coated in arousal.

How she'd feel on my fingers.

I shift my hips, pumping faster. My other hand moves up my stomach. My fingertips brush against my own flat nipple, and I'm getting into this so much that the rest of the world is gone. It's just me, and my body, and the women on the screen, and I'm fucking my fist.

Soon the redhead is down on her knees, spreading open her partner's legs. The brunette leans back on the couch, her mouth falling open in a moan as the redhead licks her. Nice, long, delicious strokes.

"Yeah," I say on a grunt, my eyes locked to the screen. I am in helping hand heaven thanks to these babes. My dick is out for a joyride, and I'm so fucking happy to be on the fast-track to coming.

I picture myself sliding between the two chicks, servicing them both, eating one, fucking the other. Nothing is better than this.

Until it gets astronomically hotter when a third one enters the scene.

She has blonde hair and brown eyes, and she's divine. I have blinders on, erasing the others, because she's all I see. Sexy, strong, and completely captivating. I can't look away. Soon, she's not her anymore...she's my girl...she's Charlotte, and she's naked in front of me, and I don't see the other women. They've disappeared from my night, as I close my eyes and jerk harder and faster, and I can't fucking fight it anymore.

I'm losing this battle because it's Charlotte I see.

It's not Charlotte from yesterday afternoon, or even Charlotte from this evening. This Charlotte is new, and she's naked, climbing up on my bed, crawling to me on her hands and knees—her sexy, pouty lips, her soft, sweet belly, her strong legs, and her beautiful, hot, wet pussy.

Wet for me.

Aching for me.

She sinks down on my shaft, and that's it.

My balls tighten, my spine ignites, and I squeeze my eyes shut as shudders wrack through me, and with an epic groan, I come so goddamn hard inside Charlotte. An orgasm that just sucks me dry.

I'm panting.

When I open my eyes, Fido is at the foot of my bed, licking his paw. He drags it over his furry face, then behind his ear. He stops his post-meal bath to stare at me, a disdainful look in his beady yellow eyes.

This is the end to my Saturday night. My cat has watched me whack off to a vision of my best friend.

"Don't say a word," I hiss.

He looks away, lifting his chin haughtily.

But he'll keep my secret.

I'll keep his, too, the fucking little voyeur.

CHAPTER FOURTEEN

Let's pretend I didn't do that.

Imagine I have amazing self-control and didn't masturbate to the thought of my business partner last night.

As she orders scrambled eggs, potatoes, toast, and black coffee at Wendy's Diner the next morning, I can't help but wonder if she knows she starred in my fantasies, riding me like a cowgirl.

Then reverse cowgirl in the middle of the night, her hair spilling down her spine, my hands on her ass.

In the shower this morning, too. I went down on her then, and she tasted absolutely heavenly coming on my tongue. So, yeah. That's the thing about slippery slopes. Take that first step, and the next thing you know, you've completed a jerk-off hat trick to your bestie.

But I'm on the wagon now. Straight and narrow. Those three times worked like a charm, and I've got her out of my system. One hundred percent. Scout's honor.

She wears a short gray skirt, a purple T-shirt, and her hair is knotted in a loose ponytail. I have no clue what's on underneath, and I'm not even thinking about her bra and panties. See? I'm cured.

"And for you?" the waitress asks me.

"I'll have the same. But well-cooked, bordering on burnt for the eggs," I tell her, and she nods and walks away, past the open kitchen.

The guy at the table next to us turns the page in the *New York Post*. A prep cook slaps butter on the griddle and it sizzles. The lights shine brightly, revealing every scratch on the faded mint-green Formica table and every nick on the beige tiled floor.

This is the morning after, and as the door opens with a jingle, a quartet of dudes a few years younger than me walk in. They partied too long, and are wildly hungover—it's obvious in their eyes.

Wendy's is a stark contrast to Gin Joint's nighttime enchantment. The diner air is thick with the scent of regret. I don't know if it's coming from others, or from Charlotte.

She fiddles with her napkin.

"Head still hurt?" I ask, since she's quiet today.

She shakes her head. "Totally fine."

"Water helped?"

She nods. "Always does."

"Good. But just to be safe, we need the full hangover prevention pack," I say, since that's why I took her here. "Nothing rebounds you better after a night of drinking than diner food. It's a medically proven fact."

She manages a faint smile, and the waitress returns quickly with the coffee pot, pouring two cups. Charlotte wraps her hands around hers. "Is it now? Even though I didn't have much to drink." Her tone is lackluster.

I don't let it deter me. The more I talk, the more we banter, the better the chance we can get back to who we were before. "There was a study just last week in the Journal—"

"About last night," she begins, and the wheels of the conversation screech to a halt with those three dreaded words.

But I'm nimble. I know how to dart and dodge. I hold up a hand like a stop sign, shaking my head. "Don't worry about it."

"But—"

"No, buts. Everything is fine."

"What I'm trying to say is—"

"Charlotte, we both had some cocktails, and hey, I get it. I look better to you when you're wearing beer goggles." I wink, going for self-deprecating humor because I don't want her to feel bad in the least for what almost happened.

The corner of her lips quirks up, but that's all. She's not wearing lipstick this morning. She hardly has on any makeup. She still looks pretty. She always does, night or day, rain or shine.

"They were gin goggles, but even without them—"

I reach for her hand, wrap mine around it, and squeeze it in a nice friendly gesture. I need to reassure her. "We're friends. Nothing can change that. Nothing is ever going to get in the way of us being friends. Well, unless you marry a total douche someday. So don't do that," I say, flashing my trademark grin and trying desperately to steer this conversation away from *us*, lest she figure out what my hand has done three times in the last twelve hours.

"Don't you marry a total bitch," she says with narrowed eyes, and that's my Charlotte. She's back, and she's just like me. She's not going to let last night's weirdness in the cab derail the best relationship either one of us has ever had. Though weirdness might not be the right word. More like hardness, wetness, and hotness. Which are exactly the words I shouldn't be using as I think about her. "But the thing I wanted to say about last night is about us being friends."

"Me too!" I say, with far too much enthusiasm, but she's just uttered the magic words. *Friends. Us.* I have to latch onto them so we don't lose sight of what we are. "Our friendship is the most important thing to me, so let's just keep being friends."

Her features freeze, as if a mask has slid into place. She fiddles with her ring, and the strangest thing is, my heart seems to beat faster as I watch her play with it. She doesn't have to be wearing it now, but she is.

"Yes. Friends. That's the most important thing," she says in a monotone.

"Like we talked about last night, right?" I say, reminding her in case her gin goggles performed a blackout trick on her brain. "Binge watching TV shows, eating gummy bears or lemonheads, and drinking tequila or wine."

She nods. "Right. Absolutely," she says, and flashes me a smile that doesn't feel real.

"We should do that again. Since we can," I say, like a card player sliding chips into the pot to bet I can just be friends with her.

"Sure."

"How about tonight?" I say, upping the ante again. I am going to blow my own mind at how good I am at just being friends.

"Okay."

"My house?" Doubling down. Big time.

"Really?" She arches an eyebrow. "You really want to just hang out?"

"Of course. We were saying last night that we should."

She shakes her head, and I'm not sure if it's amusement or some sort of resignation. She takes a breath, adjusts her ponytail, and shrugs. "Fine," she says. "Friends don't let friends eat gummy bears alone. I'll bring the bears."

"I'll eat the green ones for you."

She shudders. "Hate the green ones."

"And I'll get the wine. If memory serves, you prefer a chardonnay with your bears?"

"I do, but maybe virgin margaritas tonight instead?"

I toss my napkin onto the table with a flourish. "Touched for the very first time," I say, and again, maybe I should have thought first before those words came out.

Mercifully, the waitress arrives.

"Here are your eggs," the waitress says, setting down the plates. "Well-cooked. Just like you asked for."

Those last words echo loudly as I realize what I've just done. What I've *asked for* with my cocky mouth. My big ideas. My I-can-pull-anything-off attitude.

I just invited Charlotte into my house tonight. There aren't enough sweaty basketball players in the universe for me to deal with the danger in that decision.

* * *

We spend the rest of the meal planning for the week ahead at The Lucky Spot. Neither one of us breathes another word about tonight, or last night, or our fake relationship. When we stop by The Lucky Spot and spend a few hours working before Jenny handles the Sunday afternoon shift—and before we head to the museum—we manage the slide back into being friends and business partners so smoothly, it's as if last night never happened.

But once we set foot in the museum, something changes.

Handsy Charlotte has left the building. Sure, she's still playing my fiancée, but she's not as committed to the role as she was last night. I have no clue if my mom or Mrs. Offerman can tell, but as we stare at an Edward Hopper painting, I do my damnedest to make sure no one knows.

"The painting is beautiful," Mrs. Offerman says.

"Yes, it is," I chime in.

I wrap an arm tightly around my fake fiancée, plant a quick kiss on her cheek, and say, "Like you. By the way, have I told you how pretty you look today?"

Charlotte tenses, but manages a thanks.

My mother glances at us and smiles.

Emily does not. Emily seems to have zero interest in the artwork, even though this is her intended major.

But that's okay. I'm returning to the swing of things. I'm on my game. As we wander through Chagalls and Matisses, I make witty comments, and all the women laugh, including Charlotte. When we're out at the sculpture garden, I'm confident Charlotte and I are on solid ground, and we're good enough at playing pretend.

Until Emily turns to her. "How long have you been in love with Spencer?"

Charlotte stiffens, and a burst of red splashes across her cheeks.

"I mean, were you attracted to him first before you started dating?" Emily continues. "Because you've been friends forever, right? So was it just one of those—"

"Emily, dear. Some things are personal," Mrs. Offerman says, cutting in.

The teenage girl shrugs like this is no big deal. "I'm just curious. They went to college together. I don't think it's that weird to want to know if they were into each other back then."

Charlotte raises her chin. "We've always been friends," she says, then presses her hand to her forehead. "Excuse me."

She takes off.

My mother glares at me, and all I can think is, she knows. Her eyes track Charlotte's exit through the glass doors into the museum, and instantly my mother beckons me. I close the gap. She speaks low, out of the corner of her mouth. "She's upset about something. Go after her. Comfort her."

Right, of course. Super Fiancé to the rescue. Moms always know best.

I rush after Charlotte, through the door and down the hallway, catching up to her as she reaches the ladies' room. I call out to her, but she's got her hand on the door, and she pushes it open.

The door swings shut, and I stop.

For a second.

The hallway is quiet, far removed from most of the museum traffic. I push on the door and follow her in. She's at the sink, splashing water on her face.

"Are you okay?" I ask tentatively as I walk over to her. There are three stalls in here, but they're empty. Footsteps echo then fade down the hall.

She shakes her head. I reach her, place a hand on her lower back, and gently rub. She flinches, and inches away from me.

"Are you not feeling well? Do you have a headache from last night or something?"

The door creaks, and we freeze. It closes again, but I don't hear anyone come in. The ladies' room is silent; it's just us.

She swivels around, grabs my shirt, and tugs me into a stall. "I can't fake this."

My shoulders drop. My limbs feel heavy. I've pushed her too far. "The engagement?"

"No. That's fine. The pretend engagement is fine," she says, staring straight at me. I've never seen her brown eyes so intense, like she's about to scale a sheer wall. They don't waver at all.

I knit my brow. "Then what is it?" I'm genuinely curious because if she's not talking about our pretend relationship, I have no damn clue what it is she can't fake.

Her grip tightens on my shirt. Her jaw is set. She huffs through her nostrils. I've never seen Charlotte like this. "What did I do wrong?"

"Last. Night," she seethes. Each word has its own breathing room.

"What about last night?"

Her eyes float closed, but she looks pained. She takes a deep breath and opens them. The hard edge seems to fade somewhat. "You're just pretending like it didn't happen."

"No," I say quickly, trying to defend myself. "That's not what I'm doing."

But, in fact, it is what I've done all day. It's exactly what I'm hoping to accomplish.

"It *is* what you're doing. It's what you did at breakfast. We just brushed it under the rug, and that's not me," she says, her tone fierce, reminding me of one of the very many things I admire about Charlotte—her toughness, her tenacity. "You didn't let me talk, and I need to know. I told you I'm a shitty liar, and I meant it. I'm rubbish at lying. Even last night, when I said the thing about my dad being a nurse—that was still true."

This is yet another thing I like about her—she's so damn honest.

"Okay, so what do you need to know?" I ask, and nerves don't just skitter across my skin. They fucking descend on me like flying monkeys.

The evil kind.

As if there's any other variety.

She rolls her eyes. "Are you really this dense, Spencer?"

I hold my hands out wide. "Apparently I am. Why don't you just spell it out for me? What do you need to know?"

She twists the fabric of my shirt in her hand, pulling me closer, and in a split second, the gap between us narrows. We were a foot away before—enough space to fend off the hormones. Now, they're back. Swirling. Circling. Gripping. The temperature rises once more.

"Are you not attracted to me?"

My jaw falls. My head rings. She must be crazy. "Are you serious?"

She nods. "Answer the question, Holiday. Is that what the whole 'let's just focus on being friends' thing is about?"

"You're gorgeous. You're beautiful. You're stunning," I say, rattling off compliments like a salesman on a street corner. "I also don't want to ruin our friendship. It's too important."

She shakes her head. "You still didn't answer the question."

"I said you were beautiful."

"You said that about the Hopper, too. Are you attracted to the Hopper?"

I swallow. I try to string words together, but all that exists in my head is the film reel of last night. Of what I did to her when I was home alone with my hand, and my fantasies, and all the fucking things I want to do with my best friend. Because I am wildly attracted to her—I've learned that during the last forty-eight hours. Like, stratospheric levels of attraction. Like, the power-an-airplane-around-the-world kind.

"Do I look insane?" I ask, and my voice is strained. I hate that she's asking, and I love that she's asking, and I am strung so goddamn tight right now because this whole day was supposed to be about us being friends.

"Do you really want me to answer that?"

"Yes."

"No. You don't look insane. You look annoyed. Just like me. So I guess we're both pissed."

"No. I'm not pissed," I say, and I wrap my hand around hers and uncurl her fingers, then I slam her body against mine. "I'm not pissed. I'm fucking turned on. Because I'd have to be insane not to be attracted to you," I tell her in a harsh whisper.

Her eyes light up like sparklers. Like I've said the one perfect thing. Her irises dance with mischief and joy.

"You are?" All that anger is stripped from her tone. She's soft and feathery, and that voice wafts over me and makes me want her even more. Makes me want to hear her say other things in that voice.

"Yes." I speak through gritted teeth. With my hand around her waist, I somehow yank her closer, then I drag a finger along her jawline. "But you're not supposed to be attracted to your best friend like this. That's not how it works. I'm probably going to have to get checked into a facility to deal with the amount of attraction I have for you. I'll ask them to remove it, and they'll say, 'Sorry, sir, it's spread across your entire body and we can't take it out.'"

Her smile grows wide. "Really?" she asks, but it's hardly a question, more like a statement of wonder.

Now that she's got me going, I won't back down. It's not in my nature. "Don't make me prove it," I say, egging her on.

Her eyes sparkle. "Prove it."

"Challenge accepted."

In seconds my hand snakes up her skirt, and she gasps when it registers what I'm doing. My fingertips climb up the soft flesh of her thighs, and when I reach her panties I flick my index finger across the cotton panel. They're damp, and my dick does its best impression of the Empire State Building. I groan. Never taking my eyes off her, I slide one finger inside her panties. Her shoulders shake and my blood heats as I run that finger across her wet, hot, slippery pussy. I bring it to my lips and suck off her wetness. She tastes like all my fantasies. This time, my groan echoes. It rumbles across the ladies' room, and Charlotte trembles in my arms.

She watches me lick her off my finger, and this is the moment when there is no question. When everything is clear. She parts her lips, and says, "There's something I want to prove to you, too. Tonight."

"What is it?"

Before she can answer, the door creaks open. I break apart from her, and she smooths a hand over her shirt, then her skirt. Just so she knows, so there's no fucking doubt at all, I bring my finger back to my mouth, and I suck it one more time. With my eyes locked on hers, I whisper, *so fucking hot.*

She shudders, and her lip is quivering. I brush my finger against her lower lip, then push it past her teeth. Instantly, she draws it into her mouth and sucks.

I stare at her, burning up everywhere. I take my finger out, nip the corner of her mouth, unlock the door, and back out. I give a quick wave to Mrs. Offerman.

She blinks, then fixes on a smile and waves.

I return to the family knowing one thing for certain—I have no clue what is going to happen when Charlotte comes over tonight.

CHAPTER FIFTEEN

When I open the door, I hand her a virgin margarita.

She thanks me and takes a sip as she walks inside my apartment. She's wearing jeans, black flats, and a dressy gray tank top with some kind of lacy neckline.

Dammit. She's camouflaged. I have no clue what her intentions are based on her outfit. Admittedly, I might be oversimplifying matters, but if she were wearing a short black dress and fuck-me pumps, I'd be a lot less in the dark. Then again, I'm in jeans and a black T-shirt, so I'm not sure my clothes spell Game for Anything to her, but I hope they do.

She dangles a bag of gourmet gummy bears. "Farm fresh," she says.

"Locally grown, too, I hope?"

"Of course. Within a fifty-mile radius from farm to table."

"Excellent. They better be small-batch made, too," I say, mocking the food purists of the world, glad I can at least still banter with her.

She lowers her voice to a conspiratorial whisper. "They're from Brooklyn. Of course they're small batch. Though I still don't understand why if we can send a man to the moon, they can't remove the green bears from the bag."

"It is one of life's great mysteries." I shut the door and gesture to the living room. She walks ahead of me, and I can't help myself. I stare at her ass as she crosses the hardwood floor to my couch. She gave me the license to ogle this afternoon, as far as I'm concerned.

"Along with the existence of gigantic asparagus," she quips.

"I'll never understand the need for oversize vegetables. But did you really go to Brooklyn to get gummy bears?" I ask as she settles into my beige couch. The sliding glass doors that lead to my terrace are open, and the warm June night filters in.

She shakes her head as she kicks off her shoes, and tucks her feet under her. "The store in Brooklyn that makes them opened another shop in Murray Hill. But they *are* locally-sourced, and not made with gelatin."

"Which is a basic requirement in a gummy bear." I join her on the couch, repeating what she's said over the years— she won't touch candies made with gelatin since gelatin comes from beef, and if she wanted beef in her candy she'd eat beef candy, and she's not doing that. Because that's just disgusting.

Which is why beef candy is not a thing.

I point to my laptop. "What's it going to be? Netflix? Hulu? *Castle*? Will Ferrell's latest? Rom-com? Spy flick? Sports Center to catch up on your baseball stats?"

She rips open the bag of candy, and pops a yellow bear into her mouth. It slides past her lips. Lucky bear. "How about *Castle*? Let's watch that one with the Irish mobster."

I know exactly which one she means, since we've watched nearly every episode together. I find it quickly, sending a silent thanks to, well, myself that I remembered to close out my porn last night. Fido wanders into the living room, arches an eyebrow, and meows. I'm sure in feline language he's telling her what I did, but thank God, no one has created a Berlitz translation guide yet for cat.

We settle into the rhythm that we've perfected over the years. She's at one end of the couch, burrowed into the pillows. I'm at the other, and the laptop is on the coffee table, streaming the show to the TV screen. We plow through half the bag of gummy bears, Charlotte sifting through the colors. I dive on the green-bear grenade for her. We down our virgin drinks, and at some point during the show, she puts her feet on my thighs, crossing them at the ankles.

A spark zips through me even from that, and I flash back to last night at the restaurant when she ran her foot along my leg. I briefly wonder if I have a foot fetish. I never thought I did before, but as my gaze drifts to her feet, and the candy pink toenail polish that I can't seem to stop looking at, I realize I've missed nearly every word of Castle explaining to Beckett what he thinks is the motive in this episode's murder.

I return my focus to the screen, but my awareness of her has leveled up, like I've had a shot of caffeine and now my senses are on Charlotte alert. She shifts her shoulders into the pillow, and I steal a glance, wondering if she likes to be kissed there. She brushes a strand of hair away from her face, and I want to know how much she likes having her hair pulled, if at all. Castle and Beckett are this close to finding the killer when Charlotte munches on a red gummy bear, and I become intensely curious as to how the cherry tastes in her mouth.

She pokes me in my belly with her big toe. I tense for a brief second, wondering if she can tell where my mind is and isn't. But hers is so clearly on the screen, since she's not looking away from our intrepid heroes.

I don't get it—I was sure we'd already be naked. But then, I have no barometer for reading this woman anymore. Except, based on my astute powers of observation, I'm pretty damn sure she wants a foot rub. I reach for her foot and start massaging it, having done this many times before.

As I work my way from her arch to her heel, I try to avoid the naughtiest thoughts involving her feet. No, not the ones where I suck on her toes, because I don't have that kind of foot fetish. But the ones where I hold her ankles in my hands, spread her legs, and pound into her.

My dick transforms into a two-by-four. The fucking turncoat. I swear, if my dick were a person, he'd be a narc, always spilling my secrets.

"Fuck," I mutter under my breath.

She snaps her gaze to me. "You okay?"

"Yeah. Fine. All out of my drink," I say, grabbing the glass from the table so I have an excuse to get some breathing room. "Just keep watching. I'll be right back."

"It's okay. I'll wait." She hits the pause button, and that's the last thing I need—her scrutiny as I walk to the kitchen to refill the glass I hardly want. I drag a hand through my dark hair and stare at the pitcher of margarita mix that's mocking me with its innocence. Fuck it. I grab a tequila bottle from the cupboard and deflower my drink. I bend down, yank open the freezer and root around for more ice.

For my face.

A few seconds in the icebox cools me off.

I return to Charlotte and raise my glass. "Spiked mine," I admit, then take a long, thirsty gulp.

She holds out her hand in a grabby gesture. I give her my glass, and she drinks some. "Mmm," she says.

I set the drink down, and we return to the show as they solve a murder I couldn't care less about right now. I'm not sure what to make of this afternoon's heated moment in the bathroom at MoMA, but then I'm starting to accept that I don't know what to make of a lot of what's been happening between Charlotte and me over the last few days. I wish I did have a device to read her mind, because I'd really like to know what she wants to prove to me.

When the credits roll, she turns to me. "Want to watch Nick's show?"

No! I don't want to watch TV! I want to undress you and lick every inch of you. But you're acting so damn normal, it's throwing me off.

I shrug. "Sure. I've only seen every episode twenty times. Which one do you want to see?"

"I'll find it," she says, leaning across my legs to grab the laptop and toggle through Comedy Nation's streaming app to find *The Adventures of Mr. Orgasm*. Soon enough, the familiar theme music begins, and so do the adventures. I close my eyes and let my head fall back into the couch cushions when I realize which episode she picked.

It's the one where the woman has misplaced her orgasm. She hasn't had one in a year, and she has to hire Mr. Orgasm to track down her missing climax.

It's hilarious, and Charlotte laughs incessantly through the show, and I have a sneaking suspicion what she is trying to prove by acting like we're just good buds when we both know we're dying to do the deed, because she wants it as much as I do. The clues have been in front of me all along, and maybe I've been dense up until now, but I'm not anymore. I also don't think I can wait any longer to find out if I'm right.

I reach across the couch and hit pause on the show. The din of a siren carries from somewhere else in the city, mingling with music from the bar down the street. My home has its own noise. The hum of possibility. We are teetering on something. Something I shouldn't want. Something I want desperately.

"What did you want to prove? You said at the museum you wanted to prove something to me."

She straightens up on the couch and sits cross-legged. "That we can be friends," she says matter-of-factly.

"Okay. And did we prove that somehow tonight?"

She nods, looking pleased. "Yes. We ate gummy bears, and drank margaritas, and watched TV, and did all the things we've always done."

"Why did you want to prove this?"

"Because I'm going to proposition you," she says, speaking as directly as if she were going to offer me a job. "As you may know, it's been a while for me." She pauses and meets my gaze so I know what she means. I do. Oh yes, I do. I nod. "And apparently, I'm quite attracted to you. Go figure." She shrugs, as if this is a big surprise.

I laugh. "Yeah, go figure." I make a keep rolling motion with my hand. "Do go on."

She gestures to the laptop. "I'd like your help."

"Be more specific. Pretend I'm a totally clueless guy and you need to spell it out for me," I say, trying my best to stay cool.

"Just as you propositioned me and asked me to be your fiancée for a week, I'd like to proposition you and ask you if you'd return the favor for the next week, in a slightly different way. The way where you finish what we started last night."

That was where I thought we were heading, but now that she's said it, I'm completely unprepared for the reaction in my body. I am electrified. The key has been turned in the ignition, and I race down the road of possibility of reenacting my fantasies from last night.

"Now, I know what you're thinking," she continues, and I hope to God she doesn't know what I'm thinking, which is about how she looks naked coming on my cock. "You're worried about us staying friends. That's why I said I wanted to prove something to you. We can stay friends. It won't be weird."

Oh. Sure. Yeah. I wouldn't say I was thinking that just now, but I've thought it before, so let's go with it.

"Yes, that was on my mind," I say, fibbing mildly.

"But we've made out like, what, three times already, and it hasn't changed our friendship. Right?" she says, sounding so casual and so damn convincing, but I'm pretty sure she had me at *farm fresh*, the words she uttered when she walked in the door tonight.

"Right," I say in a strong, assertive tone, like I'm banging a judge's gavel because I'm so damn certain we should screw. Now. Then many more times tonight.

"So what would you think about us kicking things up a notch during the next week?" she says, then kicks me gently.

I think that's a genius idea, and I'm ready to pounce on her and strip her naked. To fulfill all those fantasies I had last night, and all the ones she has. To give her an epic fucking orgasm or twenty to make up for months of none but the solo variety. But deals are always done best when both parties know what to expect from the get-go.

"We just need a few ground rules," I say.

"Yes. Ground rules. Like no anal, right?"

"Um. That wasn't really on my list, but I can live with that restriction," I say with a laugh.

"Good," she says, nodding, then she scrunches up her brow. "Why? What were you thinking for ground rules?"

"More like how long this will last."

"One week. Until we break up."

Clearly she's given this some thought. "Got it. Makes sense."

"Then we go back to being friends. Promise?"

"Absolutely," I say, offering a pinky even though, let's be honest, I don't do pinky swears, being a guy and all. Still, it seems the right time to start, so she twists her pinky around mine.

"That's vital," she says emphatically as we link fingers then let go. "We just slide right back into the friend zone at the end of the week."

"No sleepovers, either," I add. "Because that just makes shit weird."

"Agreed. And no weirdness. That's another one."

I nod vehemently and slice a hand through the air. "I hate weirdness. We can't have any weirdness at all."

"Also, no lying."

"Definitely on board with that."

She counts off on her fingers. "Okay. So we've got no anal, no sleepovers, no weirdness, no lying. We do this for a week, and we return to being friends."

"Anything else?"

She shoots me a look like I'm crazy. "Well, duh. There's one more thing."

"Hit me. What is it?"

She rolls her eyes. "Obviously, no falling in love," she says with utter disdain for the concept.

I can't help but scoff, too. "Of course. Like that would ever happen."

"It would so never happen."

"There's no way. Absolutely no way." We both nod once again, completely in agreement on this topic. Then she reaches for the bottom of her tank top like she's about to strip.

I hold up a hand. "Whoa."

"You're not ready?"

"First, I was born ready. Second, I'm pretty much always ready to go at a moment's notice," I say, my eyes drifting to my crotch so she gets my meaning. "And I have been incredibly ready for the last forty-eight hours." That makes her grin. "But let's, you know, turn on some music and yada, yada, yada."

She smacks her forehead. "Right. Mood. Let's get in the mood."

"Already in the mood. But call it that if you want."

She stands and holds up a finger. "I'm just going to pee first," she says, and she scurries down the hall. She heads in the direction of the bathroom attached to my bedroom rather than the one off the kitchen. I shrug. Whatever.

I click on my streaming music app, cue up some sexy, sultry numbers that remind me of the bar last night, take my wallet out of my pocket, and grab a condom from it. I toss the condom on the table, and it slips out of my fingers easily.

It's then that I realize my palms are sweating.

Holy shit.

I'm nervous.

I'm fucking nervous, and that is not acceptable. I do not get nervous before sex. I am a rock star in the sheets. I am all confidence, all skill, and all focused on the woman. Charlotte is not getting anything less than my A game. Hell, she's getting nothing less than an A-*plus* game. I take a deep breath, letting it fill my chest. I straighten my shoulders and remind myself that this is what I excel at. This is my master class. I'm going to give Charlotte the most mind-blowing pleasure she has ever experienced in her life.

I walk over to the light switch, dim the overhead slightly, and when I turn around, Charlotte is in the living room, leaning against the wall.

She wears one of my white button-down shirts and nothing else that I can see.

I freeze.

I can't breathe. I can't blink. I can't do anything but stare at her gorgeous figure. Her blonde hair curling over the front of my shirt. Her hands restless against the buttons, as if she's unsure what to do with them. Her strong legs, all bare and beautiful. The edges of the shirt covering her. I don't know if she still has on her panties, but I'm going to have a field day finding out.

Every atom inside me buzzes. I need to touch every part of her beautiful body. Kiss every inch of her skin. Lick her, taste her, fuck her.

Please her.

"Are you trying to seduce me?" I ask as I walk over to her.

"Yes," she whispers, her voice feathery. "Is it working?"

I nod. "But that's not how this works."

Enough of her setting the rules. Enough of her making decisions. This is my fiefdom. I rake my eyes over her from head to toe and watch her reaction. She breathes hard, and her eyes shine with desire. "What do you mean?"

"You're not seducing me." I brush the backs of my fingers along her cheek, taking the reins as she trembles into my touch. "I'm going to seduce you."

CHAPTER SIXTEEN

With great power comes great responsibility.

It's not classified intel that I'm well-endowed. Charlotte's already figured that out, and she hasn't even taken off my clothes yet. But here's the secret to success when you possess a much-larger-than-average-size cock. You can't just wave it around like a big bat. You've got to treat it like a baseball manager does a closer. A cock with firepower is your secret weapon, and it's worth its weight in gold if you know what to do with the rest of the lineup. Meaning, the dick should never be the star of the show.

The woman's name should be the one in lights, and you need to make her feel that way from start to finish. Warm her up right. Use all your tools—hands, fingers, mouth, tongue, words.

Fortunately, I am well-versed in all of the above, and I intend to show Charlotte all my skills.

First, words…

"I have a confession to make," I say.

"Yes?"

"I know you were trying to prove we can still be friends when we were watching TV. But I wasn't feeling very friendly toward you."

"You weren't?" she asks, the tiniest bit of worry in her eyes.

I shake my head. "I wasn't feeling the least bit friendly when I was wondering what your lips taste like tonight," I whisper, and the worry in her gaze turns to a spark of excitement. Her chest rises and falls, as if every breath is rich with anticipation of what's coming next.

I hold her face in my hands, slant my mouth to hers, and kiss her.

Like a tease. A soft, slow, lingering tease that will do exactly what I promised her a kiss would do. I brush my lips over hers, tasting her, claiming her mouth, all before I slide my tongue between her red, eager lips.

I moan when her tongue darts out to meet mine.

This isn't our first kiss, but it's the first one that's not going to stop at kissing. It's a kiss that will go the distance.

Her breasts push against the fabric of my shirt, and soon, very soon, I'm going to meet them. I'm going to get thoroughly acquainted with her gorgeous tits, and then I'll take my sweet time getting to know every inch of her body.

That's the way I kiss her. As a promise of what's to come.

Her.

Many times.

When I break the kiss, I run my thumb across her top lip, like I'm marking this territory as mine. She lets out the neediest little gasp.

"You taste like cherry candy, and tequila, and desire," I tell her, as I lower my hand to her neck, dragging my fingers along the soft, tender skin of her throat. "And now that I've tasted you, I want to see the rest of you. I want to know what you look like naked. I've pictured it non-stop for days."

"Get me naked then," she says in a plea.

"Since you asked so nicely," I say, letting my voice trail off as I slide the first shirt button out of the hole, then the next. I'm buzzing everywhere, knowing I'm not only going to see her breasts, but I'm going to touch them, feel them, kiss them. The anticipation has its own pulse, its own presence in my apartment here with us. I want to imprint this moment on my permanent memory. To never forget how it feels to take my shirt off Charlotte.

She runs her tongue over her lips. Her eyes blaze, and she trembles. She's like a beautiful bird in a cage, wings fluttering, heart racing, dying to break free.

I'm going to be the one to do it. I get to let her escape, and experience all of her.

I free another button from its prison and my fingertips brush across the swell of her tits.

She gasps, and I groan, and we both grin at the same time from the shared realization—because it doesn't take a mind-reader to tell she loves being touched by me as much as I love touching her. Even though I'm past her breasts now, I don't spread open the shirt. I'm waiting until every damn button is undone. I want the moment to be a goddamn unveiling of her naked beauty, because I know without having seen her yet that she is gorgeous everywhere.

As I reach for the final button, I drag my fingertip down her soft flesh, and she murmurs.

I slide the last button through the hole and take a step back to look at her. I'm utterly floored by the woman in front of me. She's always been beautiful, but here, tonight, with the moonlight from my balcony illuminating her as she stands against the white wall in my living room, she is more than beautiful.

She's an angel who's come to sin with me.

My shirt is half open on her, revealing a long, luscious line from the hollow of her throat, through her cleavage, down to her belly button. She wears pink lace panties, low on her hips. Reaching for the collar of the shirt, I slide the fabric down her shoulders, stopping briefly to dust a kiss on her collarbone, then along her arms, pausing to kiss her in the crook of her elbow, then all the way to her wrists.

She shrugs off the material with a happy sigh. It falls to the ground, and my chest heats to supernova levels as I drink her in. My God, undressing her is like unwrapping a gift. Undo the bow, open the top, and discover that what's inside is even better than you dreamed it would be on Christmas morning.

She is heavenly beauty.

Her breasts are round and full, and her nipples are hard little peaks, tipping up. Her belly is flat and soft, and her hips beg for my hands to grip them as I sink into her. My dick hardens to pure steel as I picture holding those hips and sliding home.

But her breasts are at the front of the line right now, and they're getting all my attention first. My hands shoot out, cupping them. She moans the second I make contact, and lets her head fall back against the wall.

"Want to know what else I've been thinking that's not so friendly?" I say in a growl near her ear as I stroke the soft flesh around her nipples.

"What else?" she asks, her voice shooting higher as I touch her.

"I've been wondering if you'll like having my mouth on your breasts as much as I know I'm going to love it." I wrench back to look her in the eyes. "Think you will?"

She nods quickly. That desperation sends hot sparks down my spine. Her response is like a dream, and that's how I want her to feel—that this night with me is better than anything she's ever imagined.

I want her reality to exceed any and every fantasy.

Especially because the Charlotte of the last few days is nowhere to be seen. The one who wanted to tease me, the one who climbed on top of me in a cab, who whispered dirty, filthy things in my ear, has left the premises. Oh, she's not far away, I'm sure. But in her place is a softer, more vulnerable Charlotte, and that's who I want tonight.

So I can lead her.

So I can show her.

So I can take her.

Lowering my mouth to one gorgeous globe, I draw that diamond peak between my lips. She lets out a little cry, and then her hands find their way to my hair, her fingers threading tightly through it as I suck on her absolutely delicious breast, then gently tug on her nipple with my teeth. I knead her soft flesh, and a flash of images flickers in my mind, of how hot it would be to slide my dick between her tits someday. They're so highly fuckable, and she's so damn sensitive just from my tongue.

I could have a field day fucking these beauties, coming all over her skin. Not tonight, though, because that would be for me. This night is all for her.

I move my mouth to her other breast, giving it the same lavish treatment, as I caress her with my tongue. Her noises are the answer to the question I asked her about whether she'd like this. She says yes in the way her breath catches with each lick and kiss.

"So you do like it as much as I do," I say.

"*Yessssssss.*"

It is a note held long and lasting in a song. A very dirty song.

I inch my way down her body, kissing her belly, flicking my tongue across her hips. She moves and moans with the path of my mouth, breathing wildly as I taste every inch of her skin.

As I draw a delicious line around her belly button, I'm intensely aware of how much I want this night to be amazing for her. I want her to feel worshipped and fucked at the same time. Traveling down her body, my tongue explores the edge of her pink, barely-there panties, flicking under the waistband as she quivers. I near her pussy, and this is the only place I want to be right now. The only fucking place in the universe. I hook my thumbs into the slim waistband of the pink lace, when she says my name.

"Spencer."

I look up.

"Will you take off your shirt?"

In one quick move, my T-shirt is gone, and her hands are on my bare shoulders, and it feels fantastic to be touched by her, even if it's only as her anchor. That's all I want to be—the one who she holds onto as I rock her world with my mouth. I inch her panties down to her thighs, savoring every second of the reveal as I take in her nudity for the first time. I swallow dryly at the first glimpse of her mound, and the light curls of hair that cover it.

Natural blonde.

I press my nose into the hair and inhale her. I am about to taste her. I am about to slide my tongue between my best friend's legs, and I've never been so fucking turned on in my life.

"Believe me now?"

"What do you mean?" Her voice sounds as if it's floating.

"That I'm attracted to you."

"Yes," she says on a pant.

"It's beyond attraction, Charlotte. I'm fucking dying to taste you, and you better not ever doubt how much I want you, with me on my knees, peeling off your panties so I can bury my face between your thighs," I tell her, and her hips shoot closer to me.

"I don't doubt it anymore. I swear I don't," she says, so damn desperate to be touched.

I kiss her once right above her clit. Her moans tell me she's an inferno.

Just like me.

I slide the lace to her ankles, and with her hands on my shoulders, she steps out of them. I raise my face, meeting her dark eyes that blaze with a lust that matches mine. No more words. No more teasing. No more waiting.

I press my hands on the insides of her thighs, widen her stance, and groan headily as I marvel at the sight before me —Charlotte's beautiful, hot, wet pussy.

And that gorgeous clit, already hard and throbbing for me.

I dart out my tongue, flicking it across her swollen clit, and she unleashes the most glorious moan I've ever heard in my life. I grip her thighs, holding on as I kiss her sweet pussy. I could go to town on her right now. I could lap her up like a crazed, hungry man. But as much as I want to devour her, I need to pace her, to learn if she likes it fast and hungry, or if she needs more build-up. Flicking my tongue across her clit, I lick her where she wants me most. Judging from the way her fingernails curl into my shoulders, she doesn't need much more than the tip of my tongue.

She tastes like sex and dreams and lust, and she's flooding my mouth with every lick. My body isn't just an inferno; it's a volcano. My veins run with lava, and my pulse beats everywhere with desire. My dick is setting world records for hardness as it strains against the zipper of my jeans.

I need to drink this woman in. I need to be coated in her. I want her wetness covering my stubbled chin, my jaw, my face. I want this slick heat on my goddamn nose.

Using my fingers, I spread her open and lick across her slick folds. She moans in pleasure. "Oh God."

That's all she says for the next few minutes as I consume her sinfully sweet pussy, learning how she likes it. She rocks into me, her hips rolling with a wildness that mirrors the staccato speed of her erratic breathing. As I slip my tongue inside her, she digs her nails into my shoulders. As I return my mouth to her clit, she bucks against me. As I slide one finger inside her tight walls, she sings.

She fucking sings.

"Oh God, oh God, oh God, oh God."

She's said little else the entire time, and it's awesome. I love her inability to form words. I love that she can't talk while she's in heaven from my tongue, and she can only manage moans.

She hits the highest note I've ever heard, and she fucks my face in a frenzy. Her hands shoot up from my shoulders to grip my skull, and she rides my face while I lap up every last ounce of her sweetness as she comes in my mouth.

She tastes better than she did in the shower.

Better than my fantasies.

She's all real, and her orgasm is spread on my lips and all over my chin.

I am so fucking happy and so incredibly horny.

I stand, and loop one arm behind her head. She's shaking. Trembling everywhere.

Then I tell her the thing I couldn't say last night in the cab.

"God, I want to fuck you so fucking badly right now."

She answers me with the three best words a man can ever hear. "I want you." Wait. I counted wrong. Five best words, because she adds two more. "I want you so much."

CHAPTER SEVENTEEN

I scoop up her warm, pliant body, and carry her to the table in my dining room. Trust me, this is not a spur-of-the-moment decision.

I've cycled through all the possible positions and chosen this one.

Missionary—though fantastic—is not going to blow her mind for our opening night. Nor can she be on top, because I need to be in control. And no way am I fucking her from behind or on all fours the first time I sink into her. I want to see her face as I fuck her. I want to watch her lips part as she flies over the cliff, and I want to see her eyes as she comes undone.

I set her bare ass gently on the edge of the wood, and her eyes widen as realization dawns on her. For a second, I want to ask if she and Bradley ever made it out of the bedroom, but the impulse fades as quickly as it appeared, because I don't care. She's mine right now, and he will never ever get his hands on this beautiful, amazing woman again. He messed it up, and I get to have her.

"Stay here," I tell her sharply, as I walk back to the coffee table to grab the condom.

"I wasn't actually planning on going anywhere," she says in a monotone, and I smile, loving that her dry humor is never far away.

When I return, I unbutton my jeans, unzip them, push them down my legs, then kick them off. In a second, those busy hands of hers are on me, tugging off my boxer briefs as she nibbles on the corner of her lip.

When she frees my cock, it salutes her. Her eyes don't just widen. They turn to moons. "Holy shit," she murmurs and clasps a hand over her mouth.

I laugh lightly then peel her fingers from her lips. "Yes, it'll fit," I say, answering the question I know is on the tip of her tongue.

"How did you know I was going to ask that?"

I don't answer her. Instead, I ask another question as I set the condom wrapper next to her on the table. "Want to know why I say that?"

"Why?"

I drag my fingers along her slippery heat. "Because you're so wet, I'll slide inside you nice and easy." Then I reach for her hand. "Now, touch my cock."

She draws an excited breath and wraps her hand around my shaft, and I groan with decadent pleasure. She runs her hand up and down my dick, and her touch ignites me. My whole body combusts as she strokes my cock. Every inch of me is ablaze with so much want. I stand between her legs, and she's perched on the edge of my table, naked and already glowing from her first orgasm, and this moment is about as fucking perfect as a moment can be.

She plays with me for another minute, her nimble fingers exploring my shaft. A rumble works its way up my chest from the soft, delicious friction of her hands. When she spreads a bead of liquid over the head of my dick, I can't take it any longer.

"Need to be inside you," I say, and I run my hands along her thighs, spreading her legs wider for me. Reaching for the condom, I gently tear open the wrapper and slide it on.

With my hips, I nudge her legs more open, and slide the head against her wetness. Her eyes roll back, and she rocks against me, seeking me out.

I loop my fingers into her hair, cupping the back of her head. "Put it in," I tell her, in a rough voice that leaves no room for argument.

Wrapping her hand around the base, she rubs the tip of my dick against her pussy, then slides it inside, inch by inch. I let her lead. Let her take me as she can. At one point, she inhales sharply.

"Does it hurt?" I ask.

She shakes her head, lets go of my dick, and wraps her arms around my neck. "No. It feels so good."

That's my cue. I ease in the rest of the way, and then still myself when I'm inside her.

Because…hell.

Heaven.

Bliss.

This is it.

Me. Right now. This moment in time.

Her wet heat is intense. Everything, everything, *everything* about this feels so incredibly good.

Her fingers thread their way into my hair. I clasp her hips and start to move, giving her time to adjust. I watch her expression, the concentration in her brown eyes as she gets used to me. I follow her cues, giving slow, lingering thrusts, until she relaxes completely, letting me fill her. Her knees fall open, her mouth softens, and she nods.

Finally she locks her gaze to mine and whispers, "Fuck me."

Two words that light up every inch of my skin.

As I fuck her, she fucks me back. I sink deeper inside and she matches me, rising up to meet me. We set a rhythm, and we are more than in synch. We mesh.

I try to take in every sensation of our first time. The flush that darkens the skin of her chest. The scent of vanilla lotion on her shoulders. Her noises, like a woman unleashed.

Her lips are swollen and parted, and they're begging to be kissed. I dip my head to her mouth, capturing her lips as I thrust into her. We kiss—rough, hard, sloppy, mixed with sighs that tell me she's in another world, but that world is right here with me.

I slide my hands under her thighs, and she raises her legs up higher.

"Wrap them around me," I tell her.

She hooks her ankles around my back. "Like that?"

"Just like that," I repeat, then close my eyes as the pressure becomes almost too much. My quads tighten, and I can only imagine how incredible it will be to come inside her. But I stave it off as she rocks up into me.

I drive harder and deeper, hitting some spot within her that trips a switch. She gasps, shuddering. She tugs me tighter with her crossed ankles, and this is it. This is how I will take her to the edge, all tight and snug around me. Beneath me. Under me. She writhes and bucks, and she starts to lose control.

"Oh God, oh God," she moans, and her noises turn feral, echoing in my ears.

Her body is like water, like fire. She is all the elements, all woman, all vulnerable, soft, strong femininity.

She cries out—a long, low, endless, gorgeous cry. She raises her face to me, clutching her hands around my neck, hunting, and searching. In a flurry, her lips are on my ear, and she whispers, as if I needed the corroboration, "I'm coming, I'm coming, I'm coming."

Like a chant.

And, fuck, I was wrong if I thought this moment couldn't get any sexier. It did. It has. Hearing her say that in my ear, hearing her tell me she's there even though I already know, is the hottest thing ever. Because she simply *had* to voice it.

I join her, fucking her hard to my own release, inside her at last.

A minute later, after our breathing settles, I brace for the awkward to set in. But it doesn't arrive. Not as I pull out, grab the condom, and toss it into the trash can. Not as I return to her and kiss her eyelids. Not as she heads to the bathroom to clean up. And not as I ask her if she wants to watch another episode when she walks back into the living room.

Still nude.

We watch Castle and Beckett attempt to solve another murder.

We return to who we were, munching on gummy bears and pouring more margaritas and guessing plot twists, until I tug her close and Charlotte Viagra kicks back in. Soon, we're going for round two, this time on my couch, and it's not long until I hear my new favorite song as she does that thing again where she moves her lips against my ear to tell me she's coming.

After, we crash, and I wake up to Fido playing the piano on my head to let me know he's hungry, Charlotte sound asleep snuggled in my arms, and the morning sun streaming across the terrace.

We've already broken our first rule.

CHAPTER EIGHTEEN

I get the Bat-Signal in the early evening after two glorious days of nearly non-stop fucking, with occasional breaks
for work and the bare minimum of sleep.

The alert comes via text as I'm running along the West
Side Highway.

*At the gym in my building. Dipstick is here. He's staring at
my ring.*

I sniff opportunity, like a dog. Bradley is why she said
yes to being my fake fiancée in the first place, to ward off
his obnoxious gift attacks, and to exact her clever revenge.
Thank god he lost her. But still, he's scum, and now I get
to rub his loss in his face.

I break right and sprint across town, dodging pedestri-
ans, guys in suits, women in dresses, construction workers,
and everyone else in New York on this glorious Tuesday
evening as I make my way to Murray Hill. Once I reach
her building, my breath coming fast, sweat streaking down
my chest, I tell the doorman I'm here to see Charlotte.
Since I'm on her list of approved-at-all-hours visitors, he

waves me in. I head to the elevator and downstairs to the gym.

I find her in seconds. She's jogging on a treadmill at a light pace, and Bradley watches her from the exercise bike as he pedals.

I lock eyes with him, give him a quick tip of the hat, and march over to Charlotte. After I hit stop on her machine, I kiss the hell out of her. She's not expecting me, but she doesn't question it. She goes with it, melting into my kiss, and soon the kiss moves from PG to PG-13. It veers into R territory when she hops off the treadmill, wraps her arms around me, and tells me to come upstairs for a quickie before we have to go to The Lucky Spot.

That's me. Captain Fiancé at your service.

As I leave, I take a gander at Bradley. He's huffing and puffing, and looks mad as hell.

I jut up my shoulders.

What can I do? The woman wants me.

* * *

The next Bat-Signal comes from my mother later that evening as I'm working in the small office at the back of our bar, surrounded by boxes of cocktail napkins and cabinets where we store our top-shelf liquor.

At first it appears as an invitation via text. *Hi dear! We have tickets for the Fiddler revival tomorrow night. Two extra. Can you and Charlotte attend? We can all go to Sardi's beforehand.*

To say I'm not a fan of musicals would be a gross understatement. In fact, I'm surprised my mom even asked, because I'm known in the family circle for my variety of unapologetic excuses for declining all invitations to anything involving song-and-dance numbers, ranging from *I'm watching paint dry, I'm busy rearranging my ties,* to *I'll be having elective dental work done instead.*

But none of these excuses makes it from my brain to my fingers to the phone, because my first thought is that Charlotte adores Broadway. I pop out of the office to find her manning the taps at one end of the counter. "Weird question," I say as I join her. "Would you want to see *Fiddler on the Roof* tomorrow? With me?"

She studies my face, then places her hand on my forehead. "You don't have a fever."

"I'm serious."

"Maybe it hasn't set in yet."

"I mean it."

"Should I take you to the ER now to get checked, or wait for the chills to start?"

I tap my watch. "The invitation expires in five seconds. Five, four, three…"

She claps. "Yes! Yes, I want to go. I love revivals. That would be amazing. I'm not even going to ask where your bag of excuses is. I'm just going to enjoy myself."

"Good," I say, and I'm stepping closer to drop a quick kiss on her cheek when I stop myself in the nick of time.

Panic flickers across her eyes, and she makes a small jerk of her head. Jenny's here, and so are waiters and waitresses on the floor, taking drink orders.

Shit.

How the hell did that almost happen? I'm not averse to PDA, but not here at work with customers, our manager, and staff circulating.

"Sorry," I mumble.

From her spot mixing a vodka tonic, the dark-haired Jenny raises a well-groomed eyebrow, but says nothing. Charlotte doesn't wear her ring here, but Jenny's reaction makes me wonder if our employees can sense the change. Like animals sniffing out a storm, do they know their bosses are banging? Can they tell, too, it's a temporary thing? Questions race through my brain—am I standing too close to Charlotte, am I staring too hard, is it completely obvious from the way I look at my business partner that I'm picturing her naked and fucking my face right now?

I shake my head, chasing off the dirty thoughts. I try to make light of my gaffe. "We almost broke another rule," I say, just to Charlotte.

"Which one?"

"The no weirdness one."

She laughs and pats my shoulder. "You're okay, Holiday. That wasn't even tiptoeing on weird." She lowers her voice and speaks just to me. "It was actually adorable, truth be told."

Ah hell, now I'm blushing. Because...

Wait.

What the hell?

I must really have a fever. I've volunteered myself for the pain and suffering of musical theater, and I've been dubbed adorable. I am not okay with this. This is not acceptable. Charlotte is so getting fucked from behind tonight so she knows there's nothing adorable about me.

I'm only manly and rugged.

"Great," I say, coolly drumming my knuckles against the bar, like my new casual attitude will resurrect my street cred. "So we'll go tomorrow. Only 'cause you want to."

My phone buzzes once more. I grab it, and my shoulders sag as I read, *The Offermans will be there too :)*

I turn to Charlotte. "It was an ambush," I say, then share the details.

Her smile never falters. "It's okay. I don't mind going with them." She leans in closer and whispers, "In fact, it's been even easier to play your fiancée the last few days."

"Why's that?"

Her voice drops even lower. "Because of the way you fuck me all night long."

A bolt of lust slams into me, and I'm ready to drag her to the office, slam the door, and screw her here at work.

But Jenny calls her over, and I return to the computer with my new wood.

As I answer emails from suppliers, it occurs to me that Charlotte's comment about being adorable should make me feel weird. But it doesn't bug me, and I ask myself why.

Maybe because Charlotte seemed so happy to see the show. Hell, taking her to Broadway is the least I can do for her, since she's pulling off a fantastic performance this week to help seal the deal on my dad's sale.

Mystery solved. I like making Charlotte happy because she's my friend, and friends help each other.

There. I teetered, but avoided breaking another ground rule.

CHAPTER NINETEEN

The reporter joins us at Sardi's. His name is Abe, his face bears a passing resemblance to a horse, and his clothes might belong to an older brother, given that they appear two sizes too large. I'm also not sure if he has a driver's license yet, or if he's even started shaving.

He snaps photos of the two families toasting and nibbling on appetizers, and I'm truly amazed at what a puff piece this feature article is going to be. Must be why the magazine assigned a cub reporter to it. But then, *Metropolis Life and Times* is known for giving the best blow jobs in the journalism business. Open up and take it all in.

The photos are technically candid, but we're all keenly aware of the lens as we order, chat, and raise our glasses as black-and-white caricatures of theater and movie stars preside from the walls of this Broadway institution. Only couples are in attendance this time—Mr. Offerman and his wife, my dad and my mom, and Charlotte and me. Ordinarily I'd tease Harper that she was banished tonight, but she's probably thrilled to sit out this required event and skip the phony "we have no clue the reporter is here" conversation.

But I get why Mr. Offerman set up the story. Pieces like this aid in the transition of a business, and showing the friendly handoff of a jewelry powerhouse as well-known as Katharine's will reassure customers. We sure look polished and spit-shined for the magazine. I'm wearing a light green button-down shirt and a pale yellow tie with cartoon pandas on it, while Charlotte looks stunning in a black short-sleeved dress with a pink ribbon cinched through slim belt loops.

"You didn't bring your daughters along tonight," I remark to Mr. Offerman as I finish an olive. "They're busy with end-of-year school stuff, I presume? Or not fans of theater?"

He waves a hand dismissively. "We only had six tickets, and it seemed more important to bring the men."

I nearly choke on the olive pit. "Excuse me?"

"My girls don't get involved in business affairs," he says, knocking back some of his scotch before signaling to the waiter for another.

"I'm not involved in my father's business, though, and you invited me," I say, pointing out the flaw in his logic.

"True, but I'm sure your opinion is more vital than, say, your—"

His remark is cut off when the reporter taps me on the shoulder. "Picture of you and Charlotte by the bar? Our society page would love one of the happy couple."

My gut twists as I stand, knowing this photo is a sham. It'll either run online tomorrow and then be out of date when we split up in a few more days as planned. Or it will never run because...well, because we won't be the "happy couple" much longer.

As we step away from the table, Charlotte shoots me a look that says she's thinking the same thing. That we're skirting the line. Our charade seemed fine at first—a plausible enough way to ensure my romantic entanglements didn't derail Dad's business deal—even though I was lying to my family. Now, it borders on bald-faced manipulation as I lie to, well, everyone, leaving a pit in my stomach.

But the end justifies the means, I remind myself as we head to the bar. When I talked to my dad this morning, he said he expected to sign the deal by the weekend, once the final bank paperwork is completed. I hate the thought that Mr. Offerman might have walked had I not fit the mold he wanted. Still, I'm starting to see myself as more of a snake oil salesman, and I don't care for this side of me.

The good part is I'll only have to lie for another few days.

The bad part is I only get a few more days of pretending.

"Smile for the camera," Abe says as we reach the bar, the sketches of Tom Hanks and Ed Asner in the background.

I wrap my arm around Charlotte and flash a grin, then steal a quick sniff of her neck. She smells like peaches. I dust a quick kiss on her cheek, and her breath catches. She inches closer, and yup, what was fake is real again, and that nagging feeling drifts away. There's heat between us. Sizzle even. The camera's got to be picking up on the sparks.

When I let go of her, I shoot a sheepish grin at the reporter. "Sorry. Can't help myself. She's too lovely."

"It's obvious you like her," he says, then lowers his camera and retrieves a notebook from his pocket. "But I can't help but wonder, when did it become exclusive?"

"Sorry?" I ask, knitting my brow.

"It's new, right? The exclusivity in your relationship?"

"Of course we're exclusive. We're engaged," Charlotte says possessively, wrapping a hand around my arm as she deflects his question.

"I can tell," the reporter says, pointing at Charlotte's rock. "I was asking, though, when it became exclusive."

A hint of red blazes across Charlotte's cheeks, and I chime in. "The engagement is relatively new, if that's what you're asking."

"Well, it must be new," Abe says, like a dog grabbing a bone, refusing to let go. "You were in last month's *South Beach Life* magazine with a Miami chef, and just a few weeks ago I believe you were seen with a celebrity trainer."

Fuck me and my playboy ways. I tense, my muscles tightening, and here it comes—the situation my father desperately wanted to avoid.

"That was just chatter," I say, as I maintain my grin. "You know how it goes."

"You mean with Cassidy? It was casual with Cassidy Winters?" he asks, inserting the adjective of his choice—*casual*—as if he can get me to agree to use it.

"No, I wasn't saying that it was casual. I was saying it was chatter. Meaning there was nothing going on," I say crisply, correcting the bold little bastard.

He nods and strokes his chin. "Got it. But that's not the case with the chef. Because in Miami last month, you were tagged in a Facebook photo that has you giving her a kiss on the cheek."

He reaches for his phone, slides his fat thumb across the screen, and shows me the photo. He had it ready and waiting. He'd called it up in advance, preparing to pounce. I shrug, my mind quickly playing out scenarios. Then I go for it. I pucker up and give Abe a quick air kiss on the cheek. I fight every instinct to cringe as my lips come within millimeters of his baby face, but I've got to pull this off. "See? I'm just an affectionate guy."

He wipes his palm across his cheek. "So it was nothing with the chef?"

I nod and gesture to his face. "Just like that was nothing," I say, wishing I could give him the brush off he deserves. But if I walk away, or say 'no comment,' it will just fuel him. Answering coolly gives me the greatest chance of diffusing this bomb.

Abe anchors his attention to Charlotte. "Does it bother you that up until a few weeks ago, Spencer Holiday was in the papers as a noted New York City playboy?"

She shakes her head and smiles sweetly. "No. I know who he comes home to at night."

"Not every night," the reporter mumbles.

Anger lashes through me. That's the end of Mr. Nice Guy. "Excuse me? What did you say, Abe?" I ask pointedly, because it's one thing to be pushy. It's entirely another to be an asshole.

He raises his chin. "I said, so every night you'll be running The Lucky Spot as husband and wife?"

Liar.

But the liar makes a good point, and his remark reminds me that Charlotte and I are going to need a game plan for managing this fake engagement at work during the next few days. Or maybe not, since it'll be over soon.

Once again, that thought churns my stomach.

Before I can answer Abe's inquiry about how we'll run our business, Mrs. Offerman joins us, inserting herself into the impromptu interview. "Everything okay?"

I never thought I'd think this, but, boy, am I glad to see her.

"Just catching up on how quickly Charlotte and Spencer became exclusive," the reporter says to Mrs. Offerman. "Very quickly."

She arches an eyebrow, and her curiosity seems to set in. "Is that so? I knew it was fast, but wasn't aware it was *quite so recent*."

Turns out I'm actually not happy to see her. Not at all. Especially since she says those words like they're poisonous.

Charlotte clears her throat, pushes a strand of hair behind her ear, and meets Mrs. Offerman's gaze, then Abe's. "It is recent, as we've said many times. Everything happened quickly. But that's sometimes how it goes when you fall in love, isn't it?" Charlotte says as she runs her fingertips along the sleeve of my shirt. There's a layer of cotton between us, but I swear her touch ignites my skin, leaving a trail of sparks in its wake. She tilts her face and meets my gaze. My breath catches when she locks eyes with me, and briefly the rest of the restaurant ceases to exist.

I nod, swallowing dryly as I do. I'm not sure who my answer is meant for—her, them, or us.

But my yes *feels* honest at the very least, and that matters to me.

Charlotte rises on tiptoes and brushes a soft kiss to my lips. When she pulls away, she hooks her arm through mine and stares at the reporter. "It's not a problem that he was seen with someone else a few weeks ago. Doesn't change a thing. It doesn't change how I feel for him."

Abe has no more questions. At least for tonight, she's managed to throw him off the scent of our charade.

I flash back to our playful revenge on Bradley at her building gym the other night. Sure, Charlotte got a kick out of the show we staged for her ex, but that kiss on the treadmill to make him jealous was nothing compared to what she just finessed for me. She keeps saving me, again and again.

My heart trips over itself in a race to get closer to her.

Something is happening. Something strange and completely foreign. My heart is speaking a language I don't understand as it tries to fling itself at Charlotte.

Great. Now, that's two organs I have to do battle with every day.

* * *

When it's time for the show, my father commandeers my attention on the brief walk across Forty-fourth Street to the Shubert Theater entrance.

"Everything okay?"

"Absolutely fine," I reply, because the last thing I want is for him to worry. A cab screeches by, spewing out exhaust, then slams on its brakes at the red light. "The reporter was annoying, but nothing I haven't heard before."

My dad shakes his head. "I meant with Charlotte. Everything okay with her?"

"She's fine," I answer with a smile, glad that my dad cares more about the woman than the story.

He points to Charlotte, walking several feet ahead of us with the others. "You two are perfect for each other. Don't know why I didn't see it before, but now as I see you to-gether, it's like it was right in front of me all along."

Like a hawk swooping down from the sky, the guilt re-turns. This time it plants claws in my chest, settling in for a long stay. I shove my hand through my dark hair. My fa-ther is going to be so disappointed when Charlotte and I break up. "You're such a hopeless romantic," I say.

He laughs as we slow our pace when we near the crowds milling outside the brightly lit marquee. "That's why I run a jewelry store."

"Not much longer, though," I point out playfully. "You're a free man soon."

"I know." He sighs, a wistful note in the sound. "I'll miss it."

"You'll be happy to be retired, though."

He nods several times, as if he's bucking himself up. "I'll be happy to spend more time with your mom. She's the center of my world. Like Charlotte is for you," he says, clapping me on the back.

Yeah, weirdness. It's happening now for sure.

CHAPTER TWENTY

The usher seats us.

Charlotte crosses her arms, and heaves a sigh.

"You doing okay?"

She nods. Her lips form a straight line.

"You sure? Because if I were a betting man I'd say you're pissed."

"I'm fine."

I arch an eyebrow skeptically. "Are you sure nothing's wrong?"

"Nothing's wrong." She uncrosses her arms, grabs my shirt sleeve, and shifts gears instantly. "When are we going to make a voodoo doll for that reporter?"

I pretend to stare thoughtfully in the distance. "Let's see. I've got that on the calendar for tomorrow at three. That still work?"

She nods vigorously. "You bring the pins; I'll get the cloth."

"Excellent. I'll find an instructional video on YouTube so we can do it up right."

She beams, then whispers to me as the overture begins, "I hated those questions."

"He was trying to play hardball, and it's such a pointless topic. You did great though."

"They were embarrassing," she says, then beckons me closer as fiddle notes carry across the audience. "Do you think he's onto us?"

"It felt that way, but I think he was just lobbing questions to see which stuck."

"Did you like my final answer, though?"

Like it? I loved what she said about things happening quickly. More than I should. "It was fantastic."

"I did good with that one, didn't I?" she says, blowing on her fingers like she's too hot to handle.

My heart plummets, then craters to the floor. That sinking feeling comes with the recognition that I wanted some truth to what she said. I wanted something in it to be real.

"It was thoroughly believable," I say, managing a smile that is fake, and her answer is a reminder that even though for some unknown reason I don't want this to end, Charlotte is over and out in four more days.

She'll be done, but I'll want to keep this up.

The first number begins, and I think—no, I'm sure— that this is officially my least favorite time at a musical, ever. Watching it hurts.

* * *

Charlotte is quiet as we wander through Times Square, having said good night to my parents and the Offermans. We thread our way through the crazy crowds in the glitzy neon of Manhattan's famous sardine tin, sort of a mosh pit meets a zoo of people in a city of millions. A man painted as a silver robot makes jerky gestures next to a top hat collecting a few coins. A guy peddling Statue of Liberty key chains bumps into Charlotte and knocks her with his elbow.

"Ow," she mutters.

"You okay?" I ask, and reach my hand to rub. Instinct, I suppose—to take care of her. But I pull my hand back. She doesn't want it, or need it. She can take care of herself.

"Yeah, I'll be fine," she says, shrugging it off. "And hey, we survived another performance."

"Of *Fiddler*?"

She shakes her head. "No." She adopts the tone of a radio announcer. "And tonight at eight p.m., we have another rendition of Happily Engaged Couple."

I wince. "Right. That one."

This is when I should make a joke. When I should reassure her. When I should tell her thanks once again.

I say nothing. I have nothing to say. A bald man with two gold teeth barks out offers to a half-nude comedy act. "Half nude, half off."

Someone shouts back, "All nude, all off?"

We pass a theater, then a T-shirt shop, and sidestep a couple in khaki shorts, white sneakers, and NYFD T-shirts. I have no idea where we're going. Honestly, I'm not even sure why we were walking on Broadway in the first place. I think we just went in a U. What is wrong with me? I can't even navigate my own city anymore.

We reach the corner of Forty-third and stop on the concrete. A bus crawls up Eighth Avenue. Tourists circle us as we stand awkwardly, facing each other. My whole life I've known what to do, how to move forward, how to meet life at every curve and bend. Tonight, I'm thrown, and I barely understand how to put one foot in front of the other.

I scratch my head.

"Um, where are we going, Spencer?"

I shrug. "Hadn't thought about it."

"What do you want to do?" she asks, clasping her hands together as if she's looking for something to do with them.

"Whatever works for you," I say, jamming my thumbs into the pockets of my jeans.

"Do you want to go somewhere?"

"If you do."

She sighs. "Should I just get a cab home?"

"Do you want to get a cab?" I ask, and I'd like to kick myself. I can't stand me right now, this indecisive, uncertain dude in a funk who is trying to take over my body. I don't know him. I don't care for him. And I didn't give him squatter's rights in my body. I'm going to have to muscle him out of the way. I hold up a hand. "Scratch that," I say with drummed-up confidence. This fake affair might be ending in a few more days, but I'm not going to mope my way through the best sex of my life. I'm going to rise to the occasion.

"Scratch what? Getting a cab?"

I shake my head and park my hands on her shoulders. "This is what I want to do right now. I want to take you back to my place. Strip you naked. Run my tongue across every inch of your skin, and then do that thing I told you I would do to you when we were in Katharine's."

Her eyes sparkle, then shine with desire. She nods eagerly. "Yes."

There. Beautiful. I grab my phone from my back pocket to order up an Uber, since catching a cab here is impossible. As I tap my details into the app, she places her hand on my arm.

"But, um, there's something I wanted to tell you first."

Oh shit. My heart pounds. She's going to end this. She's had enough. She's gotten her fill. She's saddling up for one last ride tonight, and then she's putting me to pasture.

"What is it?" I ask, and my heart feels like it's in my throat.

"Remember when we said no lying?"

"Yes." I swallow, bracing myself. The tension ties itself into knots in my chest, and I don't like this feeling. I don't want to ever feel this way. It feels like need and dependency. Like something I barely know. "Are you going to?" I spit out.

"Going to what?"

"End this?" I ask, because I can't take it anymore.

She laughs.

"It's not funny," I insist.

"It *is* funny."

"Why?"

She shakes her head. "You idiot." She grabs my shirt and brings me closer to her. My heart throws itself against my ribs. "This is what I wanted to tell you. When you asked me what was wrong before the show started, and I said nothing? That was a lie. I was jealous. Terribly jealous."

I rewind to Charlotte crossing her arms, to her making jokes about the reporter, to her being proud of pulling off the act. "You were jealous?"

"I was trying desperately not to be. That's why I let it go and made the joke about the voodoo doll."

"Why were you jealous?"

She rolls her eyes. "All those women the reporter was naming. Hearing about them made me jealous."

"Why?"

"Don't you get it?"

"No. But we've already established you need to use the ABCs with me. So go ahead. Spell it out," I say, tapping my temple and mouthing *dense*.

She blushes, then speaks softly. Her voice is barely audible above the noise of the street, the sound of the crowds, the roar of traffic. But every word is music. "Because they were with you."

My lips quirk up. "Like how I felt about Bradley when you were with him," I admit, and it feels freeing to say that. More so, to give voice to something I'd felt but barely understood at the time.

"You felt that way when I was with him?"

"Sometimes I did," I say, flashing back to those days when she was with the supreme douche. There were nights when she left The Lucky Spot early and went home with him, and my mind wandered to her. Sure, I had women to keep me busy, but now and then the green-eyed monster paid me a visit. I'd be a sap, though, to tell her all of that. I've got to protect some of my secrets. I hold up my hands. "Go figure."

"Spencer?" she whispers.

"Yes?"

"I think we broke another rule tonight."

I arch an eyebrow. "Which one? Lying?"

"Yes, but also—"

We speak at the same time. "Weirdness."

Then we laugh. Together.

"From the way you asked me to the show, to me being jealous, to the reporter being a wiener. It was all weird," she says. She gives me a knowing look. "There's only one cure for weirdness."

"Anal?"

She swats me on the shoulder. "We're not breaking that rule. Ever," she says, her eyes drifting to my crotch. "I was thinking more like doggie style."

"That's what I meant to say." I kiss her until the car arrives.

Then the rest of the way downtown.

All the way up in my elevator.

As I open the door.

And then as I strip her naked and lay her on her stomach on my bed.

CHAPTER TWENTY-ONE

Starting at her neck, I kiss my way down her body. I travel along her spine, licking a path across her sexy, beautiful back. She sighs and wriggles on the bed. She turns her head to watch me, and I near her ass. I drop a kiss on one cheek. "Don't worry. No rules being broken. And just so you know, I'm fine with having every other part of you. I only tease you when I say that."

She smiles back at me, her way of saying thanks.

"I do like the soft flesh of your ass though, and I'm going to need to spend some time here," I say, drawing a line at the bottom of her right cheek.

She raises her rear higher, inviting me to kiss her. I lick a line around the curve of her cheek, first one, then the other, and she wriggles against me, a soft little moan falling from her lips. I press my teeth against the flesh and bite gently. Her moan rises in volume.

Lust beats a path through my veins. I'm hard, ready and eager, but I won't rush things, because I'm loving every second of this. Pressing my thumbs against her cheeks, I lift up her ass and surprise her with a slow, lingering lick along her wet pussy.

She gasps. "Didn't expect that."

"I can tell. But I can tell you like it."

"I do," she says breathily.

That's all I give her of my mouth right now. Instead, I return to her legs, wanting to work her up, to get her hot and wet from all-over kisses. I run my tongue down the back of her thigh. "Every inch of you," I say softly against her skin. "I want to have marked and kissed and touched every single inch of your skin."

"I want that, too," she says on a whimper, her voice breathy, the way she gets when she's heating up. I already know her cues, her signs, the way she responds to me, and it's only been a few days. I love knowing her body, knowing her tastes.

Like this—the back of her knee is an erogenous zone. I brush my lips there, and she makes a tiny, sexy noise.

I move down her calf, and kiss her other leg all the way to her ass again. Then, I grip her cheeks, tilt her hips, and bury my face between her legs. She tastes silky and sweet as her liquid arousal floods my tongue, and her scent fills my nostrils. She rocks back into me, and my desire for her ratchets into this deep, clawing need in my chest, in my bones. All I want is all of her. I kiss her sweet pussy until she comes on my lips.

When I step away to strip, she flips over. Her lips are parted, and her eyes look glossy. Her skin glows. "Wow," she says.

I wiggle an eyebrow in response as I shrug out of my shirt.

"I think I'm addicted to your mouth," she says softly.

"Good. Because my mouth is addicted to you."

When I reach my pants, she sits up and takes over, unzipping my jeans. "I want to do it."

She tugs off my briefs, and my cock says hello to her.

She makes a sound like a purr. "Good to see you, too," she says and darts out her tongue to lick. She swirls the tip of her tongue around the head, but before I get lost in the magical world that is her wickedly wonderful lips, I move quickly. I grab her hips, and flip her over. "Hands and knees, like a good dirty girl," I tell her.

"Am I a dirty girl?"

"You are with me," I say, as I move to grab a condom.

I stop, though, to admire the beautiful sight in front of me—Charlotte, on all fours, her gorgeous ass raised in the air. I smack it once, a light crack on the side of a cheek. She flinches, but lets out a sexy little cry. "Oh God," she moans.

That sound. Her words. Her noises. This woman is a dream. She's discovering how much she likes everything with me, and I'm learning how much I adore fucking her. I bend my head to her rear and press a kiss to the spot I smacked. Then in a flurry, I grab her wrists and push them down on the bed. "Changed my mind. On your elbows. Ass up high."

She bends like a dancer, following my lead. I drag the head of my cock through her wetness. She moans and shifts closer, wanting me, inviting me, needing me. I spank her once again, and she yelps in pleasure.

I roll on the condom and sink into her. White-hot sparks shoot through my veins. The tightness, the heat—it's astonishing. I growl, low and guttural, like an animal.

"*You*," I say on a groan. "You're so sexy. I think I'm going to set up camp here all night."

She laughs and moans at the same time. "You're crazy."

"No, I'm just fucking turned on beyond anything I've ever felt," I say, my voice rough, as I start to pump.

She's silent suddenly. No, moans, no cries, no wild pants. A small but clear voice asks, "Really?"

She cranes her neck to look up at me. My God, she's all vulnerable, her eyes so trusting, her body bent in a downward slide. "Yes," I answer as I slam into her, giving her all of me. My hands clamp tightly to her hips. "I swear, Charlotte. You fucking do something to me." I pull back out of her so only the tip is in. She writhes, trying to draw me back. "You drive me wild. You make me crazy." I thrust deeply, and her breath spills out in a gorgeous moan. "I just can't get enough of you."

"Oh God, I feel the same," she says, and bends lower, lifting higher, offering more.

She's all I want. All of her, as I fuck her like this until she comes in a frenzy of sound and heated cries. My muscles tighten, my vision blurs, and my own climax seizes my body as bright, hot pleasure crashes over me.

I flop down onto the bed, and she flops next to me. Resting her head in the crook of my arm, she stays like that —hot, sweaty, and naked. Absently I run my fingers through her hair. She brushes her hand across my stomach.

"That was amazing," she murmurs. "I think that was our best ever. I'm going to give you a gold star for excellence in orgasm delivery. A statue even."

"I'd like to thank the Academy," I begin, teasing her.

She swats my chest. "So you were faking it? Fine, so was I," she says with a huff.

In an instant, I'm on my hands and knees, pinning her. "No, you were not faking it."

Her eyes taunt me. "Yes. Yes, I was."

"You weren't. But just for that comment, you're going to show me how much you like it when I fuck you." In a flash I raise her wrists over her head, and lower my arm along the side of the bed, feeling for her dress on the floor. I grab it and yank off the ribbon from the belt loops with one hand.

I wrap it around her slender wrists then around a bed post. Her eyes track my hands the whole time as I tighten the pink fabric. "Pretty in pink," I murmur, then I run my fingertip against her lips.

I locate another condom and roll it on my dick. Yes, I'm fucking hard again. How could I not be? She's tied to my bed, still wet from her first two orgasms. Of course I'm fucking erect. I spread her legs, savoring the sight in front of me—her legs in a V, her hands bound, her eyes wide open.

I wedge myself between her thighs. "Now, you're going to beg for it."

"I am?"

"You are," I say roughly. "Because you're not getting all of it until you do."

I slide in but I only give her a few inches. I lower to my elbows so I'm close to her and proceed to slow-fuck her for the next several minutes, teasing her the whole time, never going all the way in. She moans and writhes and rocks beneath me, every thrust eliciting a new sexy murmur from her.

"Say it. Say how much you want me."

"I wasn't faking it. I was joking when I said that," she says on a pant.

"Tell me how much you want it all. Tell me how much you want all of my cock."

Her hips shoot up. "I want you. I want you so much. Fuck me deep. I'm begging you," she cries, and she *is* begging, and it is exquisite to witness her desperate sexiness.

I fuck her hard and deep, until she is out of her mind with pleasure. Until her cries turn hoarse. Until her eyes squeeze shut. Until she can't stop saying my name as she falls apart once more. Multiple orgasms sound pretty damn good to me, too, so I join her, coming again with a shudder that jolts my whole body.

When I untie her, she raises a hand to my hair, drags it through, and kisses me. "I lied. *That* was the best time ever."

"It gets better every time," I say softly.

Soon, she stands and starts to gather her clothes. Spinning in a circle, she hunts for something on the floor.

"What are you doing?" I ask curiously.

"Getting dressed."

"*Pourquoi?*"

"So I can go. Isn't that the deal?"

I crawl to the edge of the bed and tackle her, arms around her waist, surprising her.

"What are *you* doing?" she shrieks.

I toss her on the mattress and tickle her.

She cracks up. "Stop it."

I don't relent. My fingertips race up her sides, making her squirm. "I'll stop if you spend the night."

"Mercy, mercy," she calls out, and she's smiling, as wide as the sea of stars in the sky.

I tug her to me, brush her hair away from her ear, and then whisper, "Will you stay?"

Her breath hitches. "Yes. You don't care if we break another ground rule?"

"We're still ahead. I mean, I don't care, so long as you don't try to kiss me the second you wake up."

"Because of morning breath, right?"

I nod. "Not yours. Just in general."

She wrinkles her nose. "Morning breath is an excellent new ground rule. I hate morning breath."

"Me, too."

"I don't have a toothbrush, though."

"I have an extra one. Never been used," I tell her.

She places her index finger on her lips as if she's weighing all the options. "But what flavor toothpaste do you have?"

A blush creeps across my cheeks.

She notices and points. "Don't tell me you use bubblegum Crest?"

I shake my head. "No. I bought the kind you like. The minty Crest."

Her eyes sparkle, and she brings a hand to her chest. It's the sweetest thing. "You bought me toothpaste."

She sounds happier than when I bought her the ring. My heart beats faster, and words start to form on my tongue. Words that reveal strange new feelings inside me. I part my lips so I can say something. Tell her how much I am starting to feel for her. How real it is all becoming.

I stop when she lowers her mouth to mine and whispers, "You really are my best friend."

Friends.

Yes. That's all she wants to be.

CHAPTER TWENTY-TWO

Harper licks lemon ice in a cone.

"This doesn't make up for Santa," she says, pointing at the treat as we leave her favorite Italian ice vendor. "But it's a good start, and you've bought my silence for another few days."

"Good. That's all I need."

"Saw the picture of you and Charlotte this morning." She nudges me as we walk along Central Park, en route to a quick softball practice with our team's star slugger, Nick. The three of us snagged the field for thirty minutes on a Friday afternoon before the actual game tomorrow. I've got my glove and bat, and Harper has her glove in her free hand.

"You really can't stay away from me online, can you?" I tease her.

"I know. It's a terrible addiction I have, my gossip fetish."

"So it ran? The one from Sardi's?" I ask, confirming what I suspected Abe would do.

"Yup."

"That reporter from *Metropolis* is such a tool."

She furrows her brow as she licks the icy treat. "Wasn't in *Metropolis*."

As we turn into the park, I ask, "Well, where was it?"

She shakes her head, bemused. "I really can't believe you don't look this stuff up about yourself."

"Believe it. I don't. Never have. Tell me."

"It was *Page Six*."

My eyes widen. *Page Six* is the big New York gossip outlet. I try to avoid *Page Six*.

"How'd that happen? I thought he worked for *Metropolis Life and Times*."

"He's an intern there," Harper says. "Abe Kaufman. I looked him up. He's in journalism school at Columbia, so he freelances for *Metropolis Life and Times* as well as *Page Six*. Looks like he sold the picture of the two of you to more gossip-centric one."

What a tenacious fucker.

I consider the benefits. If I'm seen on *Page Six* with my loving fiancée, this could be key placement for Dad for the sale. Mr. Offerman would wet his pants to see me appear like the good, solid, soon-to-be-married son of the respected businessman he's buying the store from. "What did it say?" I ask hopefully.

She stops on the path, shoves her glove at me, and whips out her phone. She clears her throat. "Ahem. Spencer Holiday, son of the founder of the well-known jewelry chain Katharine's, and creator of the popular dating app Boyfriend Material, known for its lack of photos of a certain member of the male anatomy, is betrothed to his business partner and co-owner of the popular bar chain, The Lucky Spot. Charlotte Rhodes is also a Yale graduate, and the ring on her finger is as large as Holiday's little black book. Looks like he'll have to burn that list of numbers soon, since the one-time bachelor playboy was using it a few weeks ago. Time to zip it up, Holiday! Check back on Sunday for even more juicy photos and the full story on the engagement."

Smoke billows out my eyes. I want to find that horse-faced, cub reporter and throttle him. Wait. I hate violence. I'll play dirty instead, and slather his Facebook page with so many nut shots he has to shut it down.

Not my nuts.

Just nuts. Nutscapes, preferably.

I drag a hand through my hair. "This is everything Dad didn't want in the papers." I point to the phone. "And what the hell is he going to add to this on Sunday? He kept pushing about how new it was, and asking when we started dating. Like that's interesting? But this write-up is just complete crap. Why would the reporter write that stuff? Why do they do that?"

"Because it sells, that's why. But that's not why I'm reading the piece to you."

I hand her the phone and we resume our pace. "Why *are* you showing it to me?"

"You really don't know why I read this stuff?"

"Because you like gossip?"

"You're such an idiot. I do it for you. To look out for you."

I soften for a moment. "Really? You do it for me?"

"I do. Because you don't. I look you up online to make sure there's nothing we have to deal with, and this is something we have to deal with."

I nod. "Right. We need to figure out how to spin it for Dad."

She shakes her head. "Wrong again." She stops once more underneath a magnolia tree that canopies us with lush, green branches. "Look again." She taps the screen. "Look at this picture."

I stare at the image. Abe caught the moment when I was sniffing Charlotte's neck. My face is only half-visible, but Charlotte lights up the screen, radiant and joyful. Her eyes are bright, and I swear I see of a flicker of something in them, but my mind returns briefly to her neck and the way she smelled last night. The scent memory washes over me —peaches. She smelled like peaches and dirty dreams.

Like happiness and desire all at once.

"See what I mean?"

I look at my sister and realize she's been talking to me as I've been drifting off. "What do you mean?"

She pokes my sternum with her index finger. "Don't break her heart."

I stare at her like she's crazy, but for one rare moment, Harper's blue eyes are serious. There's no joking, no teasing in them. "I like Charlotte," she adds, as we walk along the path to the fields. "I know this started as a fake thing, but it's becoming real. At least for her."

I start to say *for me, too*, but I'm too floored by her words—I'm not sure I can form my own. I was so certain Charlotte's ground rules were genuine, that her intentions were truly just for sex, and that her goal was for us to remain friends after a few fucks. But women have intuition, even my sister. They see things men don't. "Really?"

Harper rolls her eyes. Ah, my pain-in-the-ass sister is back in full force. "I know this is shocking to you, since your knowledge of love and relationships is woefully limited. You've never had a serious relationship."

"That's not true," I say as we resume our path through the park. "I went out with Amanda in college."

"Oh, well la dee dah. *Four months*. Whoa. Let me call the record books because that is soooo serious."

"It felt serious at the time."

"Spencer, this may surprise you, given the trail of destruction you leave behind, but every now and then, God knows why, a woman might develop real feelings for you when you screw her. Just be careful, especially when it's someone you care about as a friend," she says, as we reach the ball field. Nick's there already, practicing his swing.

A million questions race through my head. I want to sit Harper down and quiz her. To ask her more about Charlotte. But Harper elbows me. She licks her lips and stares salaciously at Nick. "He's so fucking hot."

I drop my bat. It hits my toes before I can jump out of the way. "Did aliens just take over your brain?"

"Look. At. Him." She's ogling my buddy, who's wearing gym shorts and a T-shirt. "His arms. Oh my God. They are the definition of arm porn. I'm going to take some pictures to stare at later."

She starts snapping photos on her phone.

"I'm calling the psych hospital. We're checking you in," I say, wincing because my stupid toe smarts now.

Nick catches her gaze and sets his bat on the ground, leaning casually onto it, like he's some kind of star ball player. "Hey, Harper. You're looking foxy."

Foxy? What the hell? Down is up and right is wrong, and New York is falling into the ocean instead of California, because why the hell is my best guy friend hitting on my sister?

Harper juts out a hip coquettishly. She waves at Nick with her fingers and bats her eyelashes. "So are you, hot stuff," she says, then winks at him before she points at his shirt. "Can you take it off? So I can get another shot."

"Oh yeah," he says, sounding like a stripper as he yanks off his T-shirt.

"Yum." She smacks her lips and mimes making a cat claw. She leans into me and whispers, "I am so going to be visiting him one-handed tonight in my fantasies."

My eyes pop out of my head, and I clasp her shoulders.

"You have to stop now. We can get you help. There are treatment centers for temporary insanity."

"There's no stopping this train," she says, tossing her glove on the ground. Shoving her Italian ice cone into my hand, she struts over to Nick, who's shirtless, his chest and abs on full display. Harper runs her fingernails down his pecs, then locks her arms around his neck.

My fists clench, not because I want to hit Nick, but because some primal brotherly protective instinct is curling through me.

"Dude. Hands off. That's my sister."

Harper swivels around. "Gotcha! That's for ruining Santa Claus for me."

CHAPTER TWENTY-THREE

It takes a while to erase the image of my sister and Nick wrapped up in each other, even if it was just a prank, but I manage.

Thanks to my new obsession.

This photo. I can't stop thinking about what Harper said about Charlotte, and I can't stop looking at that picture on *Page Six* like it holds all the clues to the universe in it.

I stare at it as I head into the Columbus Circle station, having dropped my bat and glove at Nick's apartment near the park. My head is bent over my phone as I trot down the stairs, then slip inside the downtown train. I wrap my hand around a pole while a hipster girl in green skinny pants shoves her way onto the car, sliding past the doors just before they close. She carries bags on each arm.

"Whew," she says, relieved to have made it. But the edge of a cloth bag is caught in the door, so she yanks it free and turns in a tangle, spinning around.

Something whacks my funny bone, and I cringe. "Ow."

Her hand flies to her mouth. "Are you okay? Is it my mayonnaise?"

"Mayonnaise?" I ask, as I rub my palm over my elbow while the train slaloms around a curve in the tunnel. What is it about funny bones that hurt so damn much?

"I have jars of pesto mayonnaise in this bag. I made it myself. I'm giving it to friends. Is it okay?" There's terror in her eyes as she roots around in the straw bag on her shoulder.

Pain radiates through my lower arm while she ascertains the state of her condiments. "Don't worry about me. Your mayo just attacked me, but I won't file charges," I mumble under my breath as I wince.

She looks up, realization dawning on her. "Are *you* okay?"

I nod. "Yes. Elbow matches my toe now."

"You got hit with mayo on your toe?"

"No. A baseball bat attacked my foot earlier. Apparently, inanimate objects are out to get me today," I say as the sharpness subsides. "Is your mayonnaise going to make it?"

She nods and beams as we chug into the next stop. "It will live. Sorry I hit you."

"It's okay. Hazard of big city living."

She peers at my hand. I'm clutching my phone still. The picture is splashed across the screen. "Cute couple."

"Oh. Right," I say, raising my phone.

"They look really happy together," Mayo Girl adds.

"Do they?"

She nods. "Definitely."

"What do you think he should tell her?"

She cocks her head. "What do you mean?"

"So she knows how he feels?"

She shrugs and smiles wide. "He should just tell her how he feels. If he likes her as much as pesto mayo, he should let her know that."

"I'll tell him to consider that," I say when the train reaches its midtown stop.

As I climb up the steps and exit into the early evening, I know this situation with Charlotte isn't as simple as mayonnaise, and that's not only because mayonnaise is my least favorite food.

* * *

The Lucky Spot is a zoo. There's no time to think. No time to plan. And certainly no time to figure out what to do with the strange new notions that are implanting themselves in my head.

I need to strategize this, but I don't even know what *this* is.

Being more than friends?

Feeling something real?

Finding out if she feels the same?

What is the word for this feeling? It's like my chest is a trampoline, and my heart is doing backflips on it. Only, I've never practiced them before, and if I do them again I could land on my head.

Or my ass.

Or even my face.

So yeah. With a packed bar on a Friday night, I'm not so sure I can figure out what to do with the pesto mayo feelings.

During the evening rush, I alternate between catching up on purchase orders on my laptop, telling Charlotte about the train attack, and helping out behind the bar, while in the back office Charlotte works on ideas for a new marketing campaign.

"Out of Belvedere," Jenny remarks from the counter as she waggles an empty bottle.

"I'll grab one," I say and head to the office, where Charlotte is perched on a reclining chair, wearing jeans, and a white strappy top. When I see her, I freeze-frame through images—the photo of us, the moment on the corner of Forty-third, the pesto mayo, the toothpaste, the words she said to Abe the other night. My heart slams against my rib cage, and I wonder if this crazy overtime beating is why there are books, movies, songs, poetry about people falling—

"Hey you," she says, and the softness in her tone wafts over me. But it's the sweetness that hooks me. That sweetness feels personal, and just for me.

Yes.

This *is* why there are books, movies, songs and poetry about falling for someone. I roam my eyes over her, and even though we haven't christened this office or the bar yet, and even though I want to, my thoughts aren't on sex. They're on her, and on this jumble of words like alphabet soup inside my head.

"Hey you back," I say softly. I point at the cabinet behind her. "I need a Belvedere."

"I'll grab it." She sets her iPad on the chair, stands, and reaches for the cabinet handle. As she stretches, her shirt rides up, revealing a small sliver of her back.

"You look gorgeous," I say.

She glances back at me and smiles. "So do you. Your house later? Mine?"

Maybe this is just sex for her. Maybe that's all she wants. But even so, I need to know.

"Yes. Either," I say as she opens the cupboard, and I inch closer to plant a kiss on her bare neck.

Then pain slices through me with a *thunk* as the cabinet door connects with my skull. It reverberates. It takes over my head, my body, every single cell.

I curse up a motherfucking storm, because this hurts like hell.

"Oh my God, oh my God. Are you okay?" she says in a panic, her hands on my shoulder.

My right palm covers my eye, my head roaring as the thump echoes in my skull, epicentered in my temple.

"I think you hit my head," I say, because the whack has turned me into Captain Obvious.

"Oh God." This time she whispers the words, and she's staring at me like I've lost an eye.

"What is it?" I ask, and while I'm pretty sure I'm not down to one eye, since I can still see, I suspect my face isn't pretty.

"That's the biggest goose egg I've ever seen."

CHAPTER TWENTY-FOUR

Things I learned tonight.

First, I checked the calendar. Turns out it *is* Abuse Spencer Day, and abuse occurs in threes. But it's past midnight now, so I'd like to think the threat level has downgraded to green.

But you never know.

Second, the goose egg is the largest known bump in recorded human history, but three hours of continuous ice have not only frozen my temple but reduced the swelling to pretty much nothing. However, the bruise on the side of my face is what's referred to as a "whoa, dude, that's a big-ass bruise."

That's what the guy at Duane Reade said when I picked up ibuprofen.

Third, ibuprofen has worked wonders.

But the real test comes now. There's a buzzing near the door, and it's Charlotte, since she texted me she was on her way with supplies. I turn to Fido. He's sound asleep on the couch pillow, his tongue sticking out of his mouth. "Can you answer it?"

He doesn't respond, so I drag myself off the sofa and head to the door. I press the buzzer. "Hello? Is it the world's hottest nurse that I ordered from the temp nursing agency?"

Her laugher bounces through the intercom.

"Why yes, it is, and I'm here to give you a sponge bath."

I buzz Charlotte in, open the door, and wait till the elevator creaks up the six flights then lets her off. "You're a sight for sore eyes." I watch her walk toward me.

"Don't tell me your eyes hurt, too," she teases.

"No, just this," I say, lightly brushing near my temple.

She's holding several bags, and I shut the door behind her and return to my couch. She sets the bags down on the coffee table, and studies me. Raising her fingers, she moves them close to the bruise, but doesn't touch. "Does it hurt?"

I nod.

She leans over me and dusts a kiss on my forehead.

I moan for effect. "So much. It hurts so much."

She shakes her head, then pulls back to look at me. "Seriously. How do you feel?"

I scrunch up the corner of my mouth, torn with whether to tell her the truth—*getting better*—or to go for sympathy and sex. My decision-making process lasts all of a nanosecond. "Awful," I mutter, and that earns me one more kiss.

She sits up straight, brushes her palms together, and says, "Okay. I brought you your favorite drink," she says, reaching for the bag, and showing me an airplane-size bottle of scotch. I raise an eyebrow appreciatively. "Cold sesame noodles from your favorite Chinese restaurant." She grabs a white carton, and holds it up like it's on display. I lick my lips. "Or," she begins, dipping her hand into another bag as she retrieves something wrapped in white butcher paper, "the grilled paninis you love from the bodega on the corner. Chicken and provolone, hold the mayo. Since you hate mayo."

Forget sympathy and sex. This is what I want. Her, here with me, knowing all these things. I cup her cheeks. "I want it all," I tell her.

She kisses me, but her kisses are tentative, her lips nervous. "I'm not broken," I say as I pull away.

"I just feel bad. It's my fault. I hit you with a cabinet door."

"Well, it wasn't intentional." I pause. "Or was it?"

She shakes her head. "Of course not."

"Am I that hideous to look at now?"

She rolls her eyes. "Please. You're gorgeous, as always."

"Then what is it?"

"I just feel terrible for hurting you. I want you to feel better. That's why I brought you this care package." She gestures to the goodies.

"And I appreciate it."

"Let me get you some more ice," she says, and heads to the kitchen to grab a cold pack from the freezer. When she returns, she presses it to my forehead. Gently, I swat her hand away.

"Charlotte, I've been icing it for hours. If you ice it anymore, the goose egg will reverse itself and get sucked into my brain. That's a very dangerous condition."

She narrows her eyes but relents, setting down the pack. She gestures to the bottle of ibuprofen. "Do you need any more?"

I shake my head. "I took two at ten p.m. I'm drunk on the stuff right now."

She wrings her hands. "I'm sorry," she whispers.

I push my head back on the pillow. "Am I somehow doing something that makes you think I give a shit that you whacked me? Unless this horrific bruise is going to stop you from fucking me right now, I don't care," I say loudly.

She shakes her head.

I soften my voice as I run a finger down her neck. "Then stop fussing over me. I don't want ibuprofen. I don't want ice. I don't even want cold noodles, and they're my second favorite food behind those sandwiches you brought me, hold the mayo please."

"What do you want?"

I curl my hand around the back of her head and tug her down to me. Her lips hover inches from mine. I thought I didn't want sex and sympathy. I was right on that account. I want sex and something else, though.

Sex with her. Sex with feelings. Sex with the only woman I've ever felt this way for. I whisper in her ear, "You."

She shivers against me, then slowly, playfully she moves down my body.

As she reaches the waistband of my basketball shorts, she wiggles her eyebrows. Pressing her hand against my erection, she says, "I find it amusing that your goose egg matches your dick, Spencer."

"Yeah? In what way? Not color, I hope."

"The biggest ever," she says, then tugs off my shorts and briefs. I yank off my shirt. "This will make everything better," she murmurs as she pushes my chest flat on the couch and kneels between my legs. Her eyes stay on me as she takes her time, settling in, licking her lips, getting ready.

She takes the head of my dick in her mouth, and I sigh, I groan, I moan.

This is the very definition of heaven. Look it up. Dictionary. Right there. Charlotte's lips on my cock. She teases me, swirling her tongue around the head then licking the length of my shaft. She works her way up, flattening her tongue on the underside, and heat shoots through my veins.

My hips shift, and I want her to take me all the way in, but her kisses on my dick are driving me wild. The way she licks me like I'm her favorite candy is lightning along my spine. It crackles.

She opens wider and draws me in, sucking the head, and my eyes fall closed as I rock into her fantastic mouth.

But I don't keep my eyes closed for long. I need to see her. To watch her. Her hair spills all over my thighs, her head bobs between my legs, and her lips are swollen and red as my dick slides through them.

No better image ever.

Staring unabashedly at my goddess, I thread my fingers tighter into those strands, yanking on her hair. "Take more," I whisper, urging her on, and she does, dropping her mouth lower then cupping my balls in her hand. I close my eyes and hiss, and then I can't help it. I start to move, to pump, to fuck her beautiful mouth. My hand on the back of her head pulls her closer, seeking more. My skin burns up, and I'm close to tripping that switch, to coming hard in her mouth.

"Fuck," I say on a rough groan as I pull her off me.

I can't come in her mouth. Not when I want her this much. Not when I want her to come.

"You don't like it?" she asks, worry etched in beautiful brown eyes.

I scoff. "I love it, but I want you to ride me." I reach for my wallet and a condom. "And I want you to ride me now. That's the only thing that will make me feel better."

She shucks off her clothes in seconds flat and straddles me. I reach for her hips and lower her onto my dick, thrilling at the hot, tight feel of her. She gasps as she takes me in.

"You're so wet for me. Is that all from sucking my dick?" I ask, as I move her up and down.

She nods and pants, and then she does the sexiest thing. It's like she's not even thinking about it, which is what makes it so sexy. She drags her hand over her breasts as I thrust into her. She's touching her own tits, and it's fantastic. Everything inside me sizzles. My blood runs to Mercury levels as I watch her ride me, like a gorgeous, languid cowgirl. Her hands brush down her belly, that flat, soft belly I want to lick and kiss. She moans and pants, and it is the hottest thing in the world to witness—she's touching herself as she's fucking me.

She rides me, sliding up and down on my cock, finding her friction, chasing her release.

It's like she's masturbating with my dick.

I want her to use me. To do whatever she wants with me. To have me in any way that feels good to her. Her breath hitches, her shoulders tremble, and she starts to lose control. Grabbing her hips, I urge her on. "Let go for me, baby. You're so beautiful when you come."

"I'm close, so close," she murmurs, grinding on me, taking me deep, her moans turning to cries.

I burn up all over as I watch her. I am comprised of nothing but heat. Her lips. Her mouth. Her eyes. Everything. She is my fucking everything.

Her hand flies into her hair, and she runs her fingers through it as her other hand plays with her tits. Her eyes are closed, and she's completely lost in her own pleasure. She is beautiful and breathtaking as she fucks me to the edge. Soon she's thrusting wildly on me, and now I need to be in this with her.

"Look at me," I tell her, my voice hoarse.

Her eyes flutter open. They are hazy and full of lust and passion, and something more, something that feels incredibly new and yet intensely familiar. She starts to close them again.

"Look at me." This time it's a command, rough and heated.

"But I fall apart faster when I do," she murmurs in protest, but it's more of an admission, because her gaze locks to mine as she lowers her face close to me, her hands curling around my shoulders. "And I want it to last," she says on a moan. I know she's talking about sex, only I can't help but think she means something else, too. Like I do.

We are tethered. She doesn't look away, and I couldn't if I tried. In her eyes, I see everything I never knew I wanted. Now I *need* it fiercely. She whispers my name. It sounds like honey on her tongue. I snap. My balls tighten, and I need her to come now because I'm seconds away.

"Come on me," I rasp out, as my climax starts to tear through me. "Come on me now."

And she does on a wild cry, coming with me. She leans into me, her mouth near my ear. The epic chant sounds, and this one is new. "I can't stop. Can't stop. Can't stop."

It's so hot and so wild, the way she says it over and over. I love it. I love it when Charlotte comes. I love it when she's happy. I love fucking her. I love everything right now, even my goose egg, even the elbow whack, even the bat that fell on my damn toe.

She collapses on me, nuzzling my neck, kissing my ear, whispering *so good, so good* over and over.

"It's so good," I echo, though that adjective feels insufficient for what this has become.

"Everything is with you," she says, and when I wrap my arms tighter around her back, she snuggles into me.

"Every single thing," I say.

I love every goddamn thing in the universe, and I am the happiest bastard in the world right now, here, in this room, with the woman I have fallen for.

That's what this is. That's what the alphabet soup spells.

I've broken the biggest ground rule of all.

I've fallen in love with my best friend.

CHAPTER TWENTY-FIVE

The bat connects with the ball with a resounding whack, and I tag up on third, waiting, waiting, waiting to see if it lands in the outfielder's glove or sends me home.

Boom. Over the fence.

I pump a fist and shout.

Nick tosses the bat on the dirt and trots down the baseline as I run home. Watching him round the bases sends my father whooping from the makeshift dugout. Nick's homerun has put Dad's team ahead at the top of the ninth.

I hold out a hand and slap palms with our slugger as he nears the home plate. "Nice work, Grandslam," I say, since he's knocked out a few so far this season.

Once his foot hits the plate, the chorus from "Beautiful" by Christine Aguilera plays. Interesting choice. Not my first pick for Nick, but Mr. Offerman's daughter appointed herself "announcer" for the game and has been picking the tunes for hits, homers, and strikeouts. Emily holds up a blue, oval-shaped handheld speaker that's streaming music from her phone. She shakes her hips and encourages our team to rock out with her. Her sisters cheer her on from the three rows of creaky metal bleachers.

My father high-fives Nick as he walks off the field. "You're my ringer. Your check'll be in the mail," my dad jokes as we head toward the team bench near the bleachers. Charlotte waves and smiles. My heart beats faster as I look at her.

Tonight, I tell myself. I've got it all planned. I'm taking her to her favorite Italian restaurant in Chelsea, and I'm going to put my heart on the line. I'll tell her she's the one and then hope to hell that the woman in the *Page Six* photo is the one who's coming to dinner, not the woman who said she's just my best friend. I have no clue if Charlotte only sees me as a friendly fling, or if she wants more, like I do. But I know how I feel—I want her to be my best friend, my lover, and my partner. I want her to be all mine, and that's why this morning—after we brushed our teeth, of course—I asked her out on a real date.

She said yes.

The realization that I have an official date tonight with the only woman I've ever fallen in love with makes my palms sweat. I'll be going out on a limb and taking the biggest chance of all when I tell her that faking it led to making it for me. My pulse races with the rabid hope that this isn't a one-way street.

Hell, she's holding my keys, wallet and phone in her purse during the game—there's got to be room for the old ticker, too, right? I break away from Nick, run up the stands, and give Charlotte a quick kiss. Her lips glide across mine, and she sighs softly. In seconds, Ciara's "Pucker Up" blasts from Emily's speaker. Damn, that girl is fast.

I head down the bleachers.

Another player from the Katharine's team steps up to the plate, and my dad cheers him on. Dad's in a good mood today, not only because we're winning, but because the papers were signed this morning. His attorney is doing a final review, and filing them with the business authorities on Monday. By then, if all goes well, Charlotte and I will be a real couple, so we won't even need to break up. Amazing, how everything is coming together perfectly.

As I grab a spot on the bench, Nick speaks to me in a low voice, pretending he's talking to Charlotte. "Oh hey, Char. How's it going? You still enjoying dating Spencer? What's that? You love his big ego. Oh yeah, it's so huge. I love it, too." He turns to me, his voice deadpan. "So how am I doing at going along with things?"

I pretend to gaze in wonder. "Amazing. It's almost as if you make shit up for a living." Then I drop the snark. "And, incidentally, I'm hoping it won't be pretend much longer."

He raises an eyebrow in a question.

I shrug happily and speak quietly. "It was fake. It became real for me. I hope for her, too. I'm going to talk to her tonight and see if she feels the same."

Nick offers a fist for knocking. "Go for it," he says, no teasing, no sarcasm now. "You two always seemed right for each other."

"Yeah? Why?" I ask, eager for corroboration.

But, he laughs and shakes his head. "Dude, what do you think I'm going to say?" He clasps his hands together and bats his eyes, overdoing the hearts and flowers. "Oh, it's so sweet the way you finish each other's sentences, and both like gummy bears." He drops the act and shrugs. "All I know is you've got my vote."

"Thanks, man. I appreciate it." I pause, then narrow my eyes. "Incidentally, if you ever touch my sister, that's grounds for me to shave your head in the middle of the night and dye your eyebrows orange."

His eyes widen and he clutches his locks. "Not the hair. It's where all my power comes from."

"Exactly. So, beware."

We take our spots on the field for the bottom of the ninth, and when the other team doesn't score, "Raise Your Glass" by P!NK commemorates this Saturday-morning victory. I trot off the field and high-five my teammates.

I slap palms with Mr. Offerman. "This is going to be all yours now," I joke, gesturing to the team.

"Can't wait," he says. "I love it all. I hope you'll stay on the team, and your friend, too. We'll need a big bat if we want to win the championship next season."

Man, it's a weekend softball league. Chill out.

"I hope you win it all," I say, staying cordial through the end, as P!NK sings about all the underdogs, and Emily mimes holding a glass to go along with the words of the song. As I stuff my glove and hat into a duffel bag, I glance at Charlotte, who's getting into the celebration, too, bumping hips with Harper, and it's pretty cool to see her like this with my sister. It feels like this could be a regular thing—Charlotte hanging out with my family as the woman by my side, not just as my friend. I can picture it all unfolding before me. Days and nights of her. Real instead of fake.

The music stops abruptly, and P!NK's unbridled enthusiasm for celebrating is replaced by a tinny echo, like when someone cues up a new song with a scratch of a record.

But it's not music that comes from the handheld speaker that Emily clutches.

It's voices.

Or, rather, my voice.

"Are you not feeling well? Do you have a headache from last night or something?"

I freeze.

My blood rushes cold, as the memory of when I'd said those words slams into me with stark clarity—in the bathroom with Charlotte at MoMA. My jaw clenches and my chest seizes up, because I know what's next. My eyes search the crowd that gathers near home plate. It's sparse, but all the key players are here. The Offerman clan. My parents. Me. Like statues, listening to Emily's recording of my private conversation with Charlotte.

"I can't fake this."

The words came from Charlotte a week ago. Adrenaline kicks in, the drive to stop this right now. I take a step closer to Emily and gesture for the speaker as my voice reverberates, amplified from days ago. *"The engagement?"*

My father's brow furrows. He meets my eyes, and a flash of disappointment appears in his, chased by embarrassment.

Mr. Offerman stares at me, then snaps his gaze to Charlotte on the bleachers. Her mouth is open, and her eyes are full of terror.

Must. Stop. Now.

I rush to Emily. Maybe I can grab the speaker from her hand and hit stop before the next words sound.

"Stop it. Please," I plead, reaching for her phone, her speaker, her sense of motherfucking privacy.

She shakes her head and holds the speaker high, as the next line from Charlotte rings loud and far too clear. *"No. That's fine. The pretend engagement is fine."*

Emily hits stop, and I expect her to turn to me and say "caught you."

But instead, Abe appears, walking around the edge of the makeshift bleachers to join Emily on the field. I do a double take, and point at him. He stands next to Emily, and smiles at her like a proud...teacher?

Emily stares at her dad. "Do you believe me now that I don't want to study art at Columbia?"

Columbia. Emily's going to the same school as the tenacious reporter. That must be how she knows him.

Mr. Offerman's nostrils flare as he steps forward. "Emily, now is not the time to discuss your intended major. What on earth is this about?"

Yeah, I'm kind of wondering the same thing.

Especially because I thought this was about Charlotte and me—but it also seems to be about a father and a daughter.

Emily glares and parks her free hand on her hip. "I have no interest in studying art. I've told you that for years. You never listen to me. You never listen to what I want. I want to study business in college. Like you did. But you think business is a man's world. You're wrong, though, because I just saved you from selling your business to a liar. Ever since I met them, I knew something was off," she says, gesturing wildly to me, then to Charlotte. "So I talked to Abe at dinner at McCoy's, since we realized I'm going to the same college he attends. And guess what? He felt the same way about the happy couple, and we decided to work on it together to get to the bottom of this business deal, and the heart of the story. And it's this, Daddy."

She points at me, the accused. "Spencer Holiday faked his engagement to Charlotte Rhodes so you'd buy Katharine's, thinking it would appear like the family friendly and wholesome business you want it to be, not something associated with someone best known for discussing dick pics in the business trades." Her feet are planted wide, her hands on her hips, determination in her eyes. "How does that sound for a story that Abe can run tomorrow? Got an official press comment?"

Abe and Emily both stare at us with smug delight, but I zero in on Emily.

Mostly, I want to laugh and claim she's making all this up because the little pathological liar is off her meds. But some small part of me wants to applaud the girl for her guts. I don't like being the target of her underhanded tactics, but holy fucking balls. Emily has some big gonads, and she's sticking it to her father for being a sexist pig. She's also been playing all of us—that flirting at dinner was never flirting. She was playing me, trying to get to the bottom of the lie she sniffed out.

"Is this true?"

The question doesn't come from Mr. Offerman. It comes from my father. The man I admire. The man I respect. The man who taught me to be better than I've been for the last week. Shame washes over me as Dad sidesteps Mr. Offerman. He's not looking at the man on the other side of the business deal. He's looking at his son.

His flesh and blood who lied to him. Who embarrassed him. Who hoodwinked everyone here.

My face burns. The fact that my feelings for Charlotte have become real is meaningless. None of that matters. I nod and start to fashion an answer.

But the slap of flip-flops on flimsy metal interrupts me. Charlotte races down the makeshift bleachers and across the grass and dirt.

"Stop," she says, holding up a hand. She's twisting her ring on her finger. "The fake engagement is my fault. Don't blame Spencer."

My father furrows his brow, and turns to her. "What do you mean?"

"It was my idea," she says, contrition in her tone, guilt in her eyes. "I asked Spencer if he'd pretend to be engaged to me so my ex would stop bothering me so much." Her voice is heavy. She tugs at the ring, and I grit my teeth, hating to see it come off her finger.

"That's not true," I say. She's taking the fall, and I can't let her. This is my mess, and I need to clean it up.

She raises her chin. "It is true," she says, her tone firm and certain. Her eyes glare at me, and me alone. They say, *don't you dare interrupt me.* Charlotte looks to my dad, then Mr. Offerman. "It's all on me. I needed Spencer to pose as my fiancé so my ex would leave me alone. I live in the same building as him, and it's been awful since the split. Everyone knows he cheated on me, and I've dealt with their stares and looks of pity. But when he started begging me every day to take him back, I needed to do something drastic to make it stop."

Mrs. Offerman nods imperceptibly. Her eyes seem to say she understands Charlotte's plight. Charlotte is so damn convincing—but then, she doesn't have to be convincing. She just has to be honest. Nearly everything she's said so far is the truth. Even if the initial idea came from me, the rest of her story adds up.

Unlike my ruse.

"Charlotte, you don't have to do this," I say softly, just to her.

She shakes her head and speaks to the group. "No, I do have to do this. I asked him to pretend to be engaged to me so I could finally have some peace where I live. But please don't blame Spencer. The fake engagement was all my choice, and he went along with it because he's a really great guy, and he just wanted to help me. We planned everything, every detail, including how we would end it." She sighs, but holds her chin high. "After one week, and now it's been a week. So, I guess this is it." She tugs off the ring. Her eyes are darker than I've ever seen them before. Inscrutable. She looks to the others. "It was never real, but not for the reasons you think." She plunks the ring in my hand, and curls my fingers around it. "Thank you for pretending for me."

She wraps me in a hug. "I'm so sorry," she whispers, and my muscles tighten with a sick hope as I wait for more words just for me, words like, *I'd like to thank the Academy*, or *Do I get a gold star for that performance?* But they don't come, and her apology feels as real as any words she's ever uttered.

She breaks the embrace, casts her eyes to everyone else, and repeats herself. "I'm sorry."

She leaves, walking away from me. No *just kidding* comes my way, because this is all too real, and each step she takes crushes me. Like a fool, I stand frozen at home plate, my insides a churning mess of emotions as the embarrassment shifts into something worse. *Hurt.* So much damn hurt, like my heart has become bruised. She doesn't love me.

It was never real.

Mr. Offerman turns to my father. His nostrils flare. His eyes are hard. "I don't care whose idea it was. I don't do business with liars. The deal is off," he says, slicing his hand through the air.

Rihanna's "Take a Bow" plays from Emily's sound system.

I cringe, and Mr. Offerman roars at his daughter. "Enough."

On that count, we agree.

CHAPTER TWENTY-SIX

My head spins and my chest has a gaping hole in it.

That doesn't stop Harper. She pulls no punches.

"Look." Her hand clamps on my shoulder as she marches me through the park, Nick on my other side. "Your to-do list today just got a whole lot longer."

It's a good thing she's guiding me, because I have no clue where I'm going or what I'm supposed to do. My dad took off fifteen minutes ago to deal with the cratering of the most important deal of his career, thanks to me. And Charlotte is history. I tried to find her, but she's vanished in a puff of smoke. I could call her from Harper's phone, but as the reality settles in like a dead weight in my heart, I'm not so sure I'm ready for that kind of self-inflicted torture just now. *Hey, Charlotte. That's a bummer that you're not into me, but I had some ideas for our new marketing campaign? Oh, good. Glad you like my plans to sell more shots. Nachos are on you tonight.*

"Okay. What's on the to-do list?" I ask, my voice hollow. "Any chance it involves me waking up from this nightmare?"

She scoffs as she tugs me closer to avoid a skateboarder. "No. Welcome to your life, Spencer Holiday. Your big mouth has gotten you in a lot of trouble, and you need to dig yourself out of this hole."

"It's kind of the size of a black hole, though," Nick says. "Do you have a shovel that'll work on something that deep?"

I want to laugh. I really do. Instead, I scowl. "While you work on finding that shovel, maybe you can also let me know what to do about Charlotte? Seeing as I now run a business with a woman who served me walking papers on home plate."

My sister shoots me a look that could burn up asphalt. "She's not the first item on the to-do list, Spence."

"She's not?"

Harper shakes her head as the path spills out of the park and we curve onto Fifth Avenue. She points. Far in the distance. Down the avenue. "There. Ten blocks away you'll find a jewelry store. Up on the sixth floor is our father's office. You need to go see him and grovel."

My shoulders sag, and I sigh heavily. "I really fucked this up."

Nick laughs sympathetically. "You did, man. But now it's time to unfuck it."

I hold my hands out wide. A horse-drawn carriage clacks along Fifth Avenue behind us. "How does that work? I'm familiar with fucking. But unfucking—is that like pulling out early?"

Nick shakes his head. "Not exactly. It's a new scientific discovery, though. Like reverse osmosis, but instead of water, it filters out your fuck-up. Got it now?"

Harper rolls her eyes. "Guys. Focus. Now is not the time to practice one-upmanship in smartassery."

I drag a hand roughly through my hair. "All right. Let's do this. What is step one?"

Harper draws a deep breath and turns to Nick. "Should we tell him, or let him figure it out on his own?"

Nick screws up the corner of his mouth, then pushes his glasses higher. "Not sure his brain is working at full-speed today."

"Tell me what? Were you two talking about this already?"

"Yeah. Duh. When you tried to run off to find Charlotte," she says, and I wince at the reminder of how I raced off to catch up to her after Rihanna's song screeched to a halt. But the blond beauty was long gone, leaving me nursing this black-and-blue heart. Meanwhile, she has my phone, keys and wallet, so I'm operating blind.

Penniless, too.

"And what did you decide I need to do?"

"Dude, first you need to apologize to your dad for lying. You need to explain why you did it, that it came from the right place, but that it was a mistake, and you're sorry," Nick says, taking on the role of straight shooter.

I nod. "Got it. I can do that."

"Then you need to try to fix this mess," Harper says, chiming in.

"How?"

"You should ask to talk to Mr. Offerman. See if you can smooth things over."

I cringe at the thought of groveling to that asshat. "He doesn't want to have anything to do with Dad anymore."

"That's right now," Nick says. "Tempers flare in the heat of the moment. See if he cools down. You've got to try."

I nod, taking this all in, knowing they're right. "And if that doesn't work?"

They lock eyes again, then look back at me. "*You*. You're the way to unfucking it," Harper says.

"Oh shit," I say in a heavy voice as it hits me exactly how I'll have to reverse osmosis this fuckup for my Dad.

* * *

Harper gives me a ten-dollar bill. I feel like a grade-schooler clutching his allowance. "Now, only use it if you need to take a bus home, dear," she says, like a parent admonishing a child.

She gives me a shove toward the entrance of Katharine's. "Go."

I head inside, sticking out like a sore thumb with my gym shorts and ball cap. I make my way to the elevator and press the button for the sixth floor. After the doors close with a whoosh, I inhale and exhale, fighting to keep my focus on my dad. Not on Charlotte. Not on the worst words I'd ever heard in my life.

It was never real.

I don't know how I could have misread things between us so badly. I was so damn sure we not only had epic chemistry, but so much more. But that must just be the cocky bastard in me, making assumptions that the woman wanted me.

When the woman doesn't lie.

She made that clear from the start.

She said she's a terrible liar, which means everything she said at the ball field was true.

How the hell am I supposed to go back to working by her side? To running a business with her?

When the elevator reaches my dad's floor, the doors slide open. I step out and see a familiar face. Nina walks toward me, dressed in a crisp suit even on a Saturday. But then, Saturdays are the store's busiest days.

"Hey there. Are you looking for your dad?"

I nod. "I am. Is he in his office?"

"Yes. He's working on some contracts."

A flicker of hope ignites in me. Maybe the deal is back on. Maybe the kerfuffle blew over in mere minutes. Maybe there are Walmarts on Jupiter.

Still, I have to ask. "Is Mr. Offerman in there?"

"No," she says with a small smile, then drops a hand gently on my arm. "But go see him."

She leaves, and I draw a deep breath, square my shoulders, and walk to my father's office. Whatever is coming— whether anger or disappointment—I will take it like a man.

I knock, and Dad says to come in.

He's at his desk, still wearing his softball jersey, his fingers poised over the keyboard. I can't read the expression in his eyes. I seize the moment, the words tumbling out in a traffic jam.

"Dad, first of all, I owe you a huge apology. I lied to you and tricked you. And I'm sorry. You raised me better than that. I should never have pretended I was engaged, but in my defense, I thought—stupidly—that it would be the thing you needed for the deal. When I met Mr. Offerman, he so clearly didn't like my past or my 'reputation,'"—I sketch air quotes—"so I thought I could simply be engaged for a week as you finished the deal. It wasn't Charlotte's idea. It was mine. I thought I was doing the right thing and making sure that my past wouldn't be the reason your deal went sour. But instead it went sour anyway, because of me."

"Spencer," he begins, his lips twitching.

I hold up a hand and shake my head. "I should have been honest with Mr. Offerman at breakfast the next day, and I should have been honest with you. But I wasn't. You said all those nice things about Charlotte before Fiddler, too, and I felt like a schmuck for lying to you. You taught me to be better than that." I sigh and say the hardest part. "But at some point, it stopped being a lie, because even though it started as a fake engagement, it became real for me, and I fell in love with her."

The corners of his mouth curve up. "Spencer," he tries again, but I keep going, standing on the other side of his desk, my mea culpa pouring out of me.

"But that doesn't matter, because you heard what she said." My voice chokes with sadness as I recall her awful words. "She doesn't feel the same, and that's that. I'm sorry that I took advantage of you with the entire charade. And I know I can't make it up to you, but I want to try."

Then I dive into what I've realized I must do to make this right. "I know what you want most in the world—to retire and spend more time with Mom. I know that's why you wanted to sell Katharine's. I'm not asking you to hand it over to me. I'm not asking you to give me your business. But I'm volunteering my time. I'm offering to run the business for you. At no charge, of course," I say with a small laugh, because even in these moments, you need to keep your sense of humor. My dad's eyes sparkle as he listens. "I'm good at business. I might be terrible at relationships, and I clearly have no clue what women really want, and I have an ego that's far too big to fit on any city bus, but I'm a rock star at running all sorts of businesses. I'd love to make this up to you and be your substitute teacher while you take your time off and we find you another buyer."

I take a breath, and even though I never wanted to run the store, and even though he never intended for me to do so, it feels good to man up and make the offer. To let him know that I'm willing to fix my mistakes.

Dad rises, walks around his desk, and crosses his arms. He stands with his heels digging into the carpet of his office, his dark eyes taking me in.

The weird thing is, he doesn't look pissed.

CHAPTER TWENTY-SEVEN

"You're right, Son. I'm not happy you lied. I'm not happy you made up a whole pretend engagement. And I'm not happy you felt you had to be anything other than yourself in order for me to have what I want." He stops to squeeze my shoulder. "But I did raise you right, because to do what you just did is all I could ask for."

"I'm glad to do it, Dad," I say, and soon it will start to feel true. I'll pour my heart into it, because God knows, I need to get my mind off Charlotte. Maybe I'll even let her buy me out of the bar so I won't have to see her anymore. Seeing the woman who broke my heart every day will sting like a yellow jacket with rabies.

Dad claps my back, then tugs me in for a hug. "You're a good guy. I'm proud of you for owning up to this, and for trying to fix it." He lets go, parks his hands on my shoulders, and sighs happily. "But I'm not going to let you."

I knit my brow. "Why not?"

He laughs. His eyes twinkle. "Because you saved me. Because I was racking my brains when it was my turn at bat, trying to figure out how to get out of this deal gracefully. I was having second thoughts about selling to that pompous, chauvinistic pig in the first place, and you gave me the perfect out." He points to his paper shredder on the floor, and brushes one palm against the other. "Good thing the papers weren't filed."

A smile spreads across my face, the first one I've felt since Charlotte chopped up my heart, julienned it, and ate it for a snack.

Fine, maybe that's dramatic. But the organ in my chest is pulverized. My dad's grin, however, doesn't hurt. "He really was a pig," I say, with a quirk in my lips.

"He was completely disrespectful to women, to his wife, to his daughters—I can't have the Katharine's legacy carried on by someone like that."

"No, you can't. Leave it to us for a little bit longer as we find a better man, or woman, to sell it to," I say, and a burst of pride courses through me. I'm proud of my dad for making this choice.

He clucks his tongue. "Here's the thing. I already found someone."

My eyes widen. "You did?"

"Yes. Not to sell it to." He stops to roam his eyes over the office and then to the door, as if he's reflecting on all that's beyond. "But to run this place while I kick back. I'm not ready to let Katharine's go, even if I am completely ready to work less."

"Okay." I ask tentatively, "Who is it?"

But the instant the words make landfall, I know who it is. Something in my head clicks, like a lock sliding into place. I snap my fingers. "Nina! You asked Nina to take over day-to-day operations?"

He nods and beams. "And she said yes." He taps his finger against the papers on his desk. "That's what I was working on when you came in. Her new contract. She'll be CEO of Katharine's, and I'll remain as founder and owner while I sail across the seven seas with your mother."

"You are such a romantic," I say, shaking my head in admiration. "She's perfect for it. She's been with you from the start, and no one knows the business better."

"Exactly," he says, then strides over to his couch by the window overlooking midtown Manhattan. "But since I am a hopeless romantic, and since I have been happily married for thirty-five years, and since I know a little something about what women want, let's talk about how you're going to win back Charlotte. I saw the way the two of you look at each other."

He pats the couch. I sink down next to him, my limbs heavy. "Love the thought. But she made it clear she's not into me."

"Hmm."

"Hmm, what?"

"Did she, though?" he asks quizzically.

"I believe her exact words were, 'It was never real.'"

"Those were her words. And generally speaking, I believe a man should pay keen attention to a woman's words. But sometimes actions speak louder, and what did Charlotte's actions tell you?"

An image of her yanking off her ring mocks me.

"That she doesn't feel the same," I say bluntly. No point mincing words. He saw the same thing.

Or maybe not. He tilts his head to the side, and raises an eyebrow. He shakes his head. "I saw a woman who put her heart on the line for you."

I stare at him. His words don't compute.

"I saw a woman who took the fall for you," he continues, gesturing from him to me. "You and I both know that Charlotte didn't ask you to be her fiancé. You asked her. She said yes to you. She wanted to help you. And today, she wanted to help you, too. It might not have worked the way she intended, but she was trying to save this deal because she cares about you. She was trying to help you stay out of trouble by throwing herself under the bus."

Something comes alive inside me again.

Not an alien, or anything weird like that, but a racing heart, a spiking pulse, a thrilling possibility.

"Holy shit," I say under my breath, cycling back through the day, the morning, last night. The sandwiches, the noodles, the whiskey. The broken rules, the jealousy, the pure, private moments of bliss and connection. Last night, and the way she said she was falling. How she looked when she was naked on top of me.

I grab the collar of my T-shirt and tug. Whoa. It's hot in here. Not my brightest move to linger on a sex memory.

I shove it aside.

Most of all, I rewind to how she was always saving me from me. From the very start of this affair, right through to the end, she saved the day when I needed her most.

"I need to find her," I say, patting my pockets. They're empty. "Oh, shit. She has my phone. And my wallet. And my keys."

"Good. Because we're not moving that fast."

"Why not? Shouldn't I just go to her place and tell her how I feel or something?"

"Or something?" He arches a brow as he mimics me. "You might know a thing or two about how to land the ladies for a night. But I know how to win one woman for a lifetime," he says, tapping his heart. "Your dad happens to be a hopeless romantic. So let the master give the apprentice some lessons in winning back a woman."

I stand and hand over the reins. "I always did kick ass in school. Teach me your secrets."

He surveys my attire. "First, we need to get you into some decent clothes."

"I don't have my wallet."

He rolls his eyes. "I bought your first onesie. I think I can spring for a nice pair of slacks now."

"Dad, that's fine and all, but can you swear to never say that word again in relation to me?" I say, as we leave his office.

"Onesie, you mean?"

I nod.

He shrugs. "I'll do my best to never discuss how adorable you looked in a little baby blue onesie."

"Dad."

"Right. You weren't adorable in it. You were manly and rugged."

Have I mentioned I have the coolest dad in the universe?

CHAPTER TWENTY-EIGHT

I look sharp. I'm rocking a pair of charcoal gray pants, a navy blue button-down, and new shoes. And...wait for it...I'm freshly showered, too. Yup. Dad took me shopping and let me use the guest shower at his home. And damn, do I clean up well.

He wouldn't let me call Charlotte though.

And yes, I *do* know her number. It's one of maybe two I have committed to memory. Hers and the Chinese food delivery joint. Instead, he called her, and inquired politely if she was still available to see me tonight. Evidently, she said yes, so he told her I would be arriving at six.

As the town car I hired pulls up to her building, I feel a bit like a teenager arriving for prom. Except I don't have a corsage, or teenage stamina. Grown past that one, thank you very much.

But the nerves are the same, and mine are sky-high. I step out of the car and head to the doorman. He buzzes her, and I wait, pacing in the entryway, checking my watch, counting the number of tiles on the floor. Three interminable minutes later, Charlotte crosses the lobby.

She wears a cranberry skirt and a black top. It's the outfit I took her ring shopping in. The fact that she's wearing it knocks the breath from my lungs. It feels like a sign. As she nears me, I take in every detail. Her hair hangs loose and beautiful down her shoulders. Her lips are red and glossy. Her legs are bare, and she wears black high heels. I'm not sure I've ever told her that those shoes are my favorite, and somehow it turns me on even more that the ones she likes wearing are the ones I like seeing her in.

I can't believe it's been only eight hours since I've seen her.

She stops in front of me. Narrows her eyes. Points. "I don't know whether to kiss you or punch you. Because I've been sending text messages all day. To my purse," she says, dropping her hand into her purse and hunting around.

She grabs my phone and thrusts it at me, and the first text I see makes me grin.

THAT WAS THE BIGGEST LIE I EVER TOLD. CALL ME.

Her jaw is set hard, and she glares at me. "Oh, and I called you several times, too, before I remembered I had your phone. I was basically messaging myself all day. You had the ringer on silent, you idiot."

"Idiot seems to be the theme of the day when it comes to me," I say, but I'm smiling because this is another reason why I love her madly. The fact that she marched up to me and called me out.

She parks her hands on her hips. "Do you even want to know what my messages said?"

"I do," I say, taking her hand and lacing my fingers through hers. God, it feels good to touch her again. It feels out-of-this-world amazing when she squeezes back, her hand fitting mine so perfectly. "But right now, I want to take you out."

"To the restaurant in Chelsea?" she asks, as we reach the door of the gleaming black town car.

"Yes, but not yet. First, I'm taking you on a themed tour of New York." I gesture to her building. "This is stop one on the Lessons I Learned in the Last Week Tour."

She arches an eyebrow, inviting me to say more.

"Right here is where I was really dense," I say.

"How were you really dense?"

"Because the day I asked you to be my fake fiancée, I actually believed I could pull it off and it wouldn't change a thing," I say, as I lift the handle of the car and hold the door for her. I watch her slide into the cool, air-conditioned backseat. She looks edible.

"Did it change things?" she asks, her voice rising on the question.

I nod as I get into the car next to her and pull the door shut. "It did."

She swallows. "What's stop two then?"

I gesture north. "A restaurant called McCoy's. Heard of it?" I ask, as the car zips uptown, weaving through Saturday evening traffic.

"I believe I'm familiar with it. I'm so curious what you learned there."

When we reach the restaurant where we had our first dinner with the Offermans, I hold her hand and escort her out of the car. We don't go inside, though. We stand under the green awning, and I touch her hair, stroking the strands that fall onto her shoulder. Her breath hitches as my fingers make contact with her skin.

"As you may recall, we were here only one week ago. We had practiced kissing on the street, and in your apartment," I say, then lean in to brush a kiss to her cheek. She trembles. "But none of those practice sessions prepared me for the lesson I learned here when you kissed me at the table."

"What lesson was that?"

"How much I liked fake kissing with you."

A grin spreads across her face. "And real kissing?"

"Even better. In fact, let me just refresh your memory of how much we both like it." I cup her cheeks and capture her delicious mouth with mine. I kiss her hard, like I'm reminding her of all that's in store for us. Her arms loop around me, her breasts press to my chest, and she melts into the kiss, making those sexy sighs and murmurs that are like a current surging through me.

Other things will be surging soon, too, if we keep this up. And while that's precisely what I want, I'm not done yet with the tour.

Twenty minutes later we roll up to Gin Joint, and I lead her into the sultry, sexy bar where she drove me wild. "This is where I was a complete idiot."

Her hand slinks up my arm, and a shudder wracks through me. "How?"

"Because of that," I say.

"Because of what?"

"Because when you touch me, it turns me on like nothing ever has in my life," I say in a husky voice as I tug her close. "Yet for some crazy reason, I thought I could resist you."

She laces her hands in my hair and whispers, "So silly." She shakes her head in admonishment, now fully playing along with the tour.

"You think that's silly, then wait 'til you hear what's next. If I were to take you to the next spot, you'd realize the height of my ridiculousness."

"I would?" she asks as I walk her to the car and the cool backseat.

"Yes. Because after I took you home that night, I returned to my house and took matters into my own hand. You rode me hard in my fantasies."

Her eyes light up with the realization, and then her fingers tap dance across my leg. "That's so hot. I want to watch someday."

"Yeah, I want to watch you do that, too." I curl a hand around her head, bring my lips to her ear, and whisper, "Three times that night. And somehow, I thought I could get you of my system that way."

"Oh, Spencer," she whispers. "I thought the same thing, too."

Our lips crash together as the driver pulls away. We kiss hungrily, erasing the hours apart, the lies, the pretending. We kiss until our lips are bruised. We kiss until we reach the next destination. The corner of Forty-third. It's six-forty-five now, and theater traffic has begun, so we don't stop the vehicle.

I point through the tinted windows. "Strangest thing happened on that corner."

"What was so strange?" she asks, her happy tone telling me she wants the answers as much as I love giving them.

"I wasn't a complete idiot that night. I made sure to tell you the full truth—that I was jealous of anyone else who'd ever had you. Which was really my way of saying I don't want anyone else to have you," I say, then brush my lips against the hollow of her throat. "Ever."

"I feel the same," she says, her smile like sunshine as she grabs her phone again, this time showing me the messages she sent right after she left this morning. "Look. Just look."

About that horrid lie.

It hurt so much to say that.

I didn't mean it.

It feels so real to me.

Do you feel it too?

I look up from the screen and press my hand to her chest, over her heart. It thunders under my hand. "Yes, Snuffalaffugus. I feel it *everywhere*."

She giggles when I use our term of endearment. "Me, too. But before we fully explore *everywhere,* I really want you to read the rest of these," she says, as she peels my hand off her chest and presses her phone into my palm.

Oh great. I just realized I'm sending all these text messages to myself. BECAUSE YOUR PHONE IS LIGHTING UP MY PURSE!

Okay. So yeah. This sucks.

You've got to know I only said that on the field to try to help. I was trying to stick to the plan. To make it all believable. I HAVE NO IDEA IF IT WORKED.

Ugh. I feel awful now. I messed things up even worse, didn't I?

I'm talking to myself. But look what I found...

Seems I have your keys and wallet, too. Hmm. You have a lot of credit cards.

I've been meaning to get a new Kate Spade.

And some Louboutins.

WHERE ARE YOU? DON'T YOU KNOW WHERE I LIVE?

I'm not relinquishing this phone unless you feel the same way. I swear if I see you and it turns out this is a one-way street, you will never get this phone back. It will die a fast, painless death by the hammer of my embarrassment.

So if you're reading these messages, it must mean only one thing.

You're crazy for me, too.

"I'm so crazy for you, too," I say, and our lips come together again.

Before the moment can turn heated, before she can climb on top of me like I want her to, we somehow make it to Central Park and the baseball field. The car idles on the path, waiting for us as I walk her to the grass.

Another game is underway—a pizzeria is batting against a shoe store chain. I pull Charlotte close to me. "But this," I say, pointing to the ground, "this is where I was a huge dumbass."

She grins. "Why's that?"

"Because right here, earlier today…" I take a breath, letting it fuel me to finally share my whole heart. "This is where the woman I love went to bat for me." She gasps when I use the *L* word. "I should have told you then that I love you. I should have said everything to you." Inching closer, I press my forehead to hers. "I should have told you I'm madly in love with you, and I want you to be mine. When you told me it wasn't real, I was devastated—"

"Spencer, I didn't mean it. I said it to try to fix things."

"I know that now. I was foolish then. But it was all for the best. Because feeling like I lost you made me realize I'd do whatever it takes to have you. Because you're the one. You've been in front of me all along, and in some ways I feel like I fell in love with you quickly, in only one week. But in other ways, I know I've been falling in love with you over time, over the years. It just took faking it for me to realize that you're the only woman I've ever loved. But more than that—you're the only woman I want to love." I brush the backs of my fingers against her cheek. Her eyes are lit with joy. I recognize the emotion because I feel it with her. "And I know that, because I want to eat the green gummy bears for you so you never have to taste them, and I want to sit through the torture of *Fiddler on the Roof* with you, and drink virgin margaritas some nights, and non-bad beer other nights, and put you in bed if you're tired and have a headache, and make love to you all night long if you don't."

Her lips part, and she sighs contentedly. She grabs at my collar, pulling me even closer. "I don't have a headache tonight. And I want to do that all night long, too. I want to do that because I broke the same rule. I'm so in love with you that I'd kiss you with morning breath, and I'll even scrape pesto mayo off your sandwiches for you if anyone serves it to you by mistake," she says, locking her gaze to mine.

"I hope that never happens." My tone is intensely serious. "Because I don't want you to have to go anywhere near pesto mayo or bad breath. But if it does, I want us to deal with both horrors together."

"Me, too," she says, then kisses me—a deep, passionate kiss that seals all these lessons I learned.

When she breaks the kiss, she raises a suggestive eyebrow. "Leftover cold sesame noodles at your house instead of dinner out?"

"You're on," I say, since I know what she wants, and I want the same thing.

"Oh, wait. There's one more thing I want you to know," she says, running her hand down the buttons on my shirt, a prelude to what we'll both be doing soon.

"What is it?"

"Remember when I thought I couldn't pull this off?"

"I remember."

"I was able to because being with you rarely felt lying. It was easy to pretend to be yours."

"Why?" I ask, gripping her hips.

"It didn't feel fake. It always felt like it was becoming real."

"It is real," I say, locking eyes with her. I am rooted to this moment—it is the new hub of Charlotte and me, and I want to see and feel and taste all of it. But I also want to taste her. Right about now. "Know what else is real?"

"What else?" she asks playfully, her tone telling me she knows where my thoughts are headed.

"How much I want you this second. It's very real. It's, like, ten inches of real," I say, leaning into her so she can feel how much I crave her.

She arches an eyebrow. "Ten? I would have guessed twelve."

"Starts at ten. Finishes at twelve," I joke as I clasp her hand and return to the town car with her. Once inside, I ask the driver to close the partition. After the tinted window clicks into place, we are cocooned.

"I'll take the ten now, please."

"Ah, so you do want an appetizer before the Chinese dinner in," I say, running my hand down her spine and over her rear, squeezing her ass.

"No, Spencer. I want dessert first."

I lift her on top of me. "Appetizer. Dessert. The main course. Let's have it all," I say, raising the fabric of her skirt, and she works open my zipper.

In seconds, I tug her panties to the side, roll on a condom, and lower her onto my shaft. We moan at the same time, then we kiss and we fuck for the next few blocks. Then we kiss hard and fuck harder as the car whips downtown, my hands tugging on her hair, her fingernails clawing my shoulders, our lips smashing together as we consume each other hungrily.

We fuck as if it's been weeks since we were together, when it's only been hours. But I'll take this…this need for another person, especially since tonight is as good as it's always been. But it's worlds better, too, because it's not ending. There's no expiration date in sight, no ground rules, and no pretending.

The night turns into a marathon of sex and sesame noodles, of food and orgasms, of laughter and more of the L-word than I ever expected to utter.

We test out the strength of my coffee table and it passes; though my knees get bruised, I don't care. A little later, Charlotte suggests a shower just for fun, and since I'm a fan of fun showers, I say yes. When she kneels on the tiles, she treats me to the best shower I've ever had in my life, and does something so intense with her tongue that I've got to remember to ask her if she can tie a knot in a cherry with it, too.

Not that it matters. I have no use for knotted cherries. But I have lots and lots of uses for her tongue. Mine, too, as I indulge in another taste of her after midnight when we get into bed.

Then, we fool ourselves into thinking we'll sleep, but instead I slide inside her as we spoon in the dark. Fido provides the harmony, purring loudly when she comes, and together they sound like a mini earthquake.

"Charlotte, I have a confession to make," I tell her as I run my fingers through her hair while she comes down from her high.

"Spit it out."

"My cat's a pervert."

She laughs. "Sounds like the three of us will get along fine then."

I think so, too.

EPILOGUE

One month later

We are the only ones at The Lucky Spot. The last drink was served an hour ago, and now we're done closing up.

I grab my keys from the office, and she shoulders her purse. "Your place or mine?" she asks playfully. Then she answers it with, "I mean, *ours.*"

Her lease runs out at the end of this month, so she moved in with me a week ago. She hogs the sheets, and I sleep naked, so that might be a problem in the winter, but aside from that, life with her is pretty much perfect. Add in the fact that Abe's article never ran, since there was no sale of Katharine's, only a fake engagement that turned into a genuine love story. I'm a happy camper and so is my dad, who's somewhere in the Mediterranean now while Nina runs the store.

The only thing that would make this moment more perfect is a bottle of wine.

"Before we leave, let's have a quick glass," I say, heading behind the bar and grabbing a bottle I picked out for the night.

She shoots me a curious look from her side of the bar. "Do you want to just have that at home?"

I shake my head. "Nope. Here."

I pour a glass for myself, then one for her. I slide it across the bar. I hold mine up to toast. "To re-creations."

She furrows her brow. "What? You're not making any sense."

"Work with me. It'll make sense soon." I take a drink, then set down my glass. "Isn't it funny how everyone thinks we're a couple?"

"But we are a couple," she says, shaking her head and tapping the glass. "Were you drinking a lot before you cracked this one open, Holiday?"

I'm undeterred. "We need a story," I say, reminding her of what she told me in her kitchen the day we first decided to fake it. "Remember?" I ask, prompting her. "One Thursday night at The Lucky Spot, over a glass of wine after closing time…"

Recognition dawns, and her brown eyes twinkle. "Yes. If memory serves, you said what you just said."

I repeat myself, holding her gorgeous gaze captive. "Isn't it funny how everyone thinks we're a couple?"

She remembers her line—her made-up, make-believe line about how we came together. "Maybe we should be one."

I say nothing. She doesn't speak either. We both recall the script, and how it called for an awkward pause.

When the pause is weighted with enough awkward, I speak, the corner of my lips curving up. "But this time, there's more after the awkward pause," I say, then dip my hand into my pocket.

"What happens next?" she asks breathily, her palms pressed on the counter, anticipation evident in how her shoulders curve toward me.

"A magic trick."

"Show me."

I leave my post and walk around the bar. When I reach her, I wave one hand behind her left ear, then I take my other hand out of my pocket, and brush it behind her right ear. "Look what I found behind your ear," I say, then open my palm in front of her.

"Oh God," she says, her voice catching.

I bend down to one knee and take her hand. "I have a proposition for you. When we first played make-believe fiancée, you used two words that we both swore we'd never hear again. But even then they sounded perfect coming from you. *Mrs. Holiday.* And that's because you're the only one I ever want to be Mrs. Holiday, and I hope you think it sounds as sexy and beautiful as I do. Will you marry me?"

"I love being propositioned by you, so the answer is... *yes,*" she says, as a tear slips down her cheek.

Never has one word been more perfect.

I hold up the ring, letting the stone catch the light from above. "This is the ring you picked out—the one you wanted, the one that's perfect for you. It's also the ring I got for you the first time, and it's the one I want you to wear for always," I say, as she holds out her hand.

"Put it on me," she says, in between happy sobs. "It's the only one I want. You're the only one I want."

I slide it on her ring finger for the second time, and I know that it will be the forever time.

ANOTHER EPILOGUE

Six months later

My wife is fucking awesome.

But don't just take my word for it. Consider all her accomplishments.

She's bright, she's beautiful, she's funny, and she married me.

End of story.

Oh, wait. There's one more thing I have to say. So, yeah. We broke pretty much all the rules. We had sleepovers, and we lied, and it was weird, and we fell in love, and it didn't last a week. It's lasting a lifetime.

There are two rules we kept though. Remember how we agreed to stay friends? We remain friends. Best of friends.

Now, you're probably wondering about that *other* rule. Charlotte held fast on that one, but I'm not missing a thing, especially considering how well she can tie cherry stems with her tongue. I'm the luckiest bastard on the face of the earth, because I'm madly in love with the woman I come home to every night. My wife. My best friend.

And I make her happy every night.

If you know what I mean.

And I think you do.

Happy wife = happy life.

THE END

COMING SOON!

Mister Orgasm!

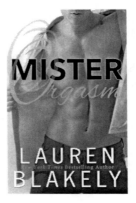

Did you enjoy getting to know Nick Hammer, Spencer's best friend? Stay tuned then for Mister Orgasm! Nick's got a story to tell too, so get ready for another dirty, cocky, funny all-guy POV when Nick tells his story! Coming in Summer 2016!

Just call me Mr. Orgasm. No, really. I insist.

Orgasms are my specialty. Delivering them. Administering them. Giving them in multiples. Then doing it again for an encore. I'm like the superhero of pleasure.

But before anyone gets all up in a lather about my "manwhore ways," remember this. You probably didn't even look at me years ago. You likely didn't give me the time of day when I was the quiet geek bent over his notebook drawing cartoons about a caped crusader bestowing orgasmic pleasure to womankind.

Now, that I'm creator of the hottest animated TV show in the world — The Adventures of Mr. Orgasm — everything has changed. The women have lined up. The checks roll in. And the life I'm living is goooooooood — looks, talent, and a masterful dong have gotten me far.

There's only one thing in my way — the woman I took home last night has turned out to be my new boss.

Oops.

Looks like the Adventures of Mr. Orgasm have only just begun...

To be notified when MISTER ORGASM becomes available, please sign up for my newsletter:

laurenblakely.com/newsletter

COMING SOON!

The Sapphire Affair

The Sapphire Affair is a two-book series about a sexy, high-end bounty hunter hired to find stolen jewels, and the only thing in his way is a gorgeous and adventurous woman who's after them too...

Both books should be available for preorder soon! Get ready for a sexy, witty, suspenseful, contemporary romance with shades of mystery and crime — Seductive Nights meets the Thomas Crowne Affair.

To be notified when *The Sapphire Affair* becomes available in summer 2016, please sign up for my newsletter:

laurenblakely.com/newsletter

Check out my contemporary romance novels!

The New York Times and USA Today
Bestselling Seductive Nights series including
Night After Night, After This Night,
and *One More Night*

And the two standalone
romance novels, *Nights With Him* and
Forbidden Nights, both New York Times
and USA Today Bestsellers!

Sweet Sinful Nights, Sinful Desire
and *Sinful Longing*, the first three books
in the New York Times Bestselling high-heat
romantic suspense series that spins
off from Seductive Nights!

Playing With Her Heart, a
USA Today bestseller, and a sexy Seductive Nights
spin-off standalone! (Davis and Jill's romance)

21 Stolen Kisses, the USA Today
Bestselling forbidden new adult romance!

Caught Up In Us, a New York Times and
USA Today Bestseller! (Kat and Bryan's romance!)

Pretending He's Mine, a Barnes & Noble and
iBooks Bestseller! (Reeve & Sutton's romance)

Trophy Husband, a New York Times and
USA Today Bestseller! (Chris & McKenna's romance)

Far Too Tempting, an Amazon
romance bestseller! (Matthew and Jane's romance)

Stars in Their Eyes, an iBooks bestseller!
(William and Jess' romance)

My USA Today bestselling
No Regrets series that includes

The Thrill of It
(Meet Harley and Trey)

and its sequel

Every Second With You

My New York Times and USA Today
Bestselling Fighting Fire series that includes

Burn For Me
(Smith and Jamie's romance!)

Melt for Him
(Megan and Becker's romance!)

and *Consumed by You*
(Travis and Cara's romance!)

ACKNOWLEDGEMENTS

Thank you to Helen Williams for the C and R and the complete and absolute cover awesomeness! Thank you to KP Simmon for rolling with the crazy. Big hugs to Kelley for running the ship. Huge gratitude to my girls, Laurelin, CD and Kristy.

A big massive smooch and kisses to Jen McCoy, the first reader to fall in love with Spencer and the one who made sure the magic all came together. I am grateful to Lauren McKellar for her keen eye, insight and attention to detail, and to Kara Hildebrand for helping me nail the prologue.

Thank you to my family and my husband, and to my fabulous dogs!

Most of all thanks to YOU – the reader. The books are always for you.

Xoxo
Lauren

CONTACT

I love hearing from readers! You can find me on Twitter at LaurenBlakely3, or Facebook at LaurenBlakelyBooks, or online at LaurenBlakely.com. You can also email me at laurenblakelybooks@gmail.com.

CPSIA information can be obtained at www.ICGtesting.com
Printed in the USA
LVOW10s0201020316

477310LV00024BD/1673/P